CONTENTS

J
GL

J

Amber Wellington, Daredevil

Amber Wellington,

Daredevil

by DIANNE GLASER
illustrated by MARVIN GLASER

WALKER AND COMPANY
NEW YORK

First published in the United States of America
in 1975 by the Walker Publishing Company, Inc.

Published simultaneously in Canada by
Fitzhenry & Whiteside, Limited, Toronto.

ISBN: 0–8027–6197–6

Library of Congress Catalog Card Number: 74–78854

Printed in the United States of America.

Designed by Robert Bartosiewicz

10 9 8 7 6 5 4 3 2 1

*Deep thanks goes to
Margery Cuyler
and
Andrea Horyczun
for encouraging me to write
and rewrite this book.
Also, a special thanks to
my optimistic husband
and
children
for spurring me on.*

Amber Wellington, Daredevil

1

The Daredevils

Ten-year-old Amber Wellington threw back the cover and sat in bed peeking out the window at Joel's house. On the second floor, his bedroom window shade was still down, so he wasn't awake yet. Good. This meant she would be the first one out to the clubhouse if she hurried. She slipped into jeans and a shirt, remembering to spread Gran's Martha Washington bedspread nice and neat, for her Gran despised a wrinkled bed. This was a special morning and everything had to go just right. Amber paused outside the bathroom door and smiled as she heard her grandmother mumuring to herself in the mirror as usual.

"Well, well, I look just like death wearing pajamas this morning," Mrs. Stone said. Actually, she didn't mean a word of it. She prided herself on her trim good looks, especially for a woman her age.

Amber walked barefoot into the large kitchen, glancing out the open back door across the back alley to check Joel's window once more. She poured herself a glass of milk as Gran rounded the kitchen corner, fully dressed and bursting with morning energy. Her high heels clicked and her jewelry jingled.

"Amber, look at me, are my lips on straight? Do I have too much eyebrow pencil on?"

"No'm, everything looks real good. Listen, Gran, I just want milk and toast this morning——" Amber began.

"What? Why that's not enough to keep a bird alive! Here's your juice and after that you run on up and wake your mother, and we'll have our bacon and eggs."

"But Gran——"

Mrs. Stone put her hands on her hips and Amber knew she really meant business.

"The most important meal of the day is your breakfast! I've always said that and you don't argue with me either, young lady!"

She began to step firmly about the kitchen and Amber's hopes went down. Now she'd be the last one at the club and all the plans would be made without her! Darn! She stomped her bare feet softly as she climbed the stairs to her mother's room.

The sound of bacon sizzling followed her as Gran began singing "Come to the Church in the Wildwood" in her customary breakfast serenade. It was a typical Saturday morning in the white frame house on Magnolia Avenue in Bluntsville, Alabama.

Amber stood at the open bedroom door and looked in at her mother sitting at the dressing table brushing her hair. She saw Leah Wellington lower the silver-handled brush and gaze at the photograph resting on the marble top dresser. It was a picture of Amber's father, Captain Robert Wellington, handsome and smiling in his uniform, his Army hat cocked at a jaunty angle.

The mirrored reflection of her mother's face was stricken with a sudden sadness and Amber immediately came into the bedroom.

She slipped up behind her and clasped her hands over Mrs. Wellington's eyes.

"Guess who, Mother?"

"Let me see, could it be Shirley Temple?"

"Good gosh, no! That sissy girl?"

"Well, is it David Harding, counterspy?"

"Nope, give up?"

"Only if you give me a good morning kiss, angel. Did you sleep well?"

Amber hugged her mother, feeling a rush of love for her. Nobody's mother was as sweet and pretty as hers, not in the whole town.

"Mother, what were you thinking about just now? Just before I snuck in?" Amber asked.

"Why, I was—honey, I was just thinking how proud your daddy would have been if he could have seen what a fine girl you're growing up to be. You must always remember him, Amber. He loved you very much."

Leah Wellington held her daughter close and they were silent for a moment.

"Gran got mad at me last night," Amber confessed as she buried her face in her mother's warm neck.

"What about?" asked Mrs. Wellington, leaning back to look into Amber's blue eyes. She reached for the brush and began to braid her daughter's long yellow hair.

"Well, I sneaked a lemon and a goodly amount of salt into her bed while I was writing in my diary, and I guess I got some salt on the sheets. Gran kept complainin' all night she felt like she was sleepin' on a bed of nails."

"Now, listen, you know Gran's not as young as she used to be." Mrs. Wellington looked disapprovingly at Amber. "You really mustn't snack in her bed. Anyway, lemons and salt? Why, that's enough to dry up your blood! I worry about you all the time for being too thin and it's no wonder, eating that kind of stuff!"

Mrs. Wellington wrapped the last rubber band around Amber's braid. "I want you to come downtown with me this morning. Dr. Gray thinks you may need braces and you have a dental appointment at eleven. You'd best change into a dress."

"But, Mother, I'm supposed to meet Joel at his house early! We have something special to do today. I hate that old dentist! Nobody goes on Saturday! Every single person I know goes to the dentist on a school day. Georgia Anne's mother gets her excused from geography class to go!"

"Well, your mother takes you on Saturday because I work at the shop and today is the only free day I have. Don't argue, Amber!" Mrs. Wellington closed the door gently and went downstairs to help with breakfast.

Grown-ups always have the last word, thought Amber in exasperation. She changed into a dress and patent leather shoes and walked slowly down the stairs. The thought of Dr. Gray's soft pink fingers in her mouth made her shiver.

"Dentist! Urp, slop, bring the mop!" she said to herself as she sat down at the table. And worst of all, what about the club?

"Breakfast is now served," said Gran rather formally, as she did every morning of the world. Amber sighed resignedly.

After breakfast, Amber and Mrs. Stone walked to the bus stop as they did each Saturday while Mrs. Wellington stayed home and washed the breakfast dishes. The feather on Mrs. Stone's hat bobbed with each brisk step she took.

She glanced at Brother Barker's house and frowned up at Joel who was grinning from his corner window. Amber grinned at him as they passed.

"Amber, that little Barker boy is nothing but a scalawag! You know what they say about preacher's sons. They're ten times as mischievous as regular boys."

She looked sharply at her granddaughter, but Amber scrutinized the cracks in the sidewalk.

"Only the good Lord knows what all that boy gets himself into," Mrs. Stone continued in the familiar lecture.

"I had a talk with Alta May and seeing as how she'll be responsible for you this summer while your mother and I are at the dress shop, I told her you're not to run wild with that Joel Barker every day. You hear that? I'm only working half a day today, you know, and when I get home, we're going to talk some more about this!"

Obediently, Amber nodded her head but in her heart she felt resentful. She wished grown-ups wouldn't fuss so about Joel. He was the smartest, most admirable person she knew, and Alta May liked him, too. Thank goodness for that.

Just then Mrs. Stone's bus pulled up to the corner. She gave Amber a good-bye peck on the cheek.

"Hey there, Mr. Gipson, I see you're running late again this mornin'," she said pertly. Mr. Gipson snorted his air brakes in irritation. Mrs. Stone mounted the steps, and the bus pulled away from Magnolia Avenue.

Amber headed straight for Joel's back door at top speed.

Amber sat contentedly at Mrs. Barker's kitchen table, watching Joel eat a plate of pancakes loaded with syrup. Between each gooey bite, he drank a large swallow of Coca-Cola.

"Yuk! How can you stand all that sweet stuff for breakfast?" she asked him, sickened yet fascinated by his meal.

Joel continued to eat, slurping loudly.

His mother smiled at them from her place at the sink. She was coring cabbages and scalding the glass Libby jars for canning. Hmmm, that raw cabbage sure did smell good, Amber thought.

"You fixing to make sauerkraut, Miz Barker? Can I have one of the cabbage hearts? And some salt?" added Amber, her jaws tingling at the thought.

"Why, you sure can, honey," said Joel's mother kindly, setting on the table a plateful of cabbage hearts and the salt shaker. Joel reached for them.

"Listen, Joel," Amber said softly. "I got to go to the stupid old dentist office. Will you wait for me? I'm gonna get initiated 'cause you promised me this Saturday for sure!"

Joel munched a cabbage stalk dipped in syrup. He whispered back, "It meets on Saturday morning only, Wellington! I told you that! The other guys

aren't gonna wait around all day for some girl and you know it!"

Amber hissed at him across the table. "Now listen here, Mr. Smart-aleck-that-can't-wait-for-anybody. I can't help it if Mother makes me, can I? It's not my fault! You're the president, and you crossed your heart and swore to stick a needle in your eye if I couldn't be in the club. Come on, Joel!"

His only answer was a loud and prolonged belch. Amber shuddered in delight. She looked quickly at Mrs. Barker, but she didn't even seem to notice. The water ran noisily in the kitchen sink.

Such a rude burp at Amber's dinner table would have never been forgiven! Boy, that Joel could get away with anything, 'cause he was the "baby of the family." She knew for a fact it was true, too, seeing as how Mrs. Barker would save him special Sunday chicken parts and never made him wear "hand-me-downs" like all his other brothers had to do. The only thing he ever wanted to wear that wasn't brand new was a black leather motorcycle jacket of Bubba's. In fact, Joel's brother, Bubba, didn't want to give it up, but his mother made him. Joel wore it even in the hot weather because he felt so big in it.

"Joel, will you wait if I fix it for you to miss church on Sunday morning and Sunday night?"

"If you can do so much, prove it!" Joel was interested, all right.

"Watch this. Oh, Miz Barker, Mother and Gran said could Joel please go with us up to the lake early tomorrow morning?"

"Why, Amber, tomorrow is church, honey. Joel's daddy is preachin' to three visiting ministers from over at Holy Oaks and he'll be wanting all his boys there on the front pew. All seven of 'em!"

"But, Miz Barker, Mama says we need Joel. She wants to make sure I don't drown or get hurt, off by myself. Oh, let him go, Miz Barker; I can't go 'less he goes, too!"

This was a plain, all out lie. Amber felt guilty.

Mrs. Barker looked undecided, then she gazed at Joel and her face melted into a smile.

"Well, I reckon he could miss just the one Sunday and it wouldn't hurt."

Amber impulsively hugged the woman's plump waist.

"Oh, boy, oh boy. Boy hidy, Miz Barker, you're so good!"

At the table, Joel's face grinned all over. He walked her out to the screened porch. "Wellington, I got to hand it to you. I'm not too proud to admit you're really somethin' when it comes to talkin' somebody round the fence and back. Listen, we'll have us a time, catchin' crawdads and water snakes."

She pulled his curly hair a sharp yank in recognition of the praise and grinned at him. At the screen door she spoke warningly, "Now remember, Joel, I'll be back here by 1:00. Don't do *anything* till I get here!"

He made a face at her, but as he nodded she knew he would wait. One thing about having a preacher's son for a friend was that they'd feel a thousand times more guilty if they lied than just a regular person. Sometimes there might be "an exception to the rule" as Gran said, but Joel usually would keep his word.

As she walked up the back alley, she noticed a tall man standing by the old dogwood tree. His flaming red hair glinted in the morning sunlight. Amber stared curiously. The man was looking down at a mewling, scrawny cat. She drew a quick breath in surprised anger as she saw him draw his leg back and kick viciously. A loud shriek rang out and the cat's lean spotted body went flying through the air.

It landed on its thin legs and raced away into the bushes. The cruelty of the red-headed man's action maddened Amber.

She began to walk faster. Larnie's cafe had all kinds of weirdos passing in and out. She'd better hurry up. Her mother was counting on her to go to that rotten dentist's office.

She got home just in time. Her mother was all dressed, even had her "rat" in her hair and everything. Amber couldn't understand for the life of her why ladies called that roll of fake hair in the hairnet a "rat!" It sure was a horrible name for a mighty pretty looking hair style.

When they got on the bus, Amber sat up nice and straight. She was glad to be sitting next to Mrs. Wellington who smelled so good of perfume and fruity chewing gum.

Amber tried not to think about the dreaded trip to the dentist and turned her thoughts to that all-important meeting at the club this afternoon. At last, at last, she was getting into the Daredevils! She'd be the very first girl allowed in it, too, thanks to Joel.

Besides Amber, there was only one other girl on their block. Her name was Carey and her folks were so strict she was scared to do a single thing unless she checked it out with them first and then they always said no. Carey didn't have a prayer of being a club member, not as long as she lived.

The other club members were boys and all of them lived on the same block as Amber. All but one. He was the new boy. Everyone called him Pig but his real name was Richard Brooks and he said he could open Coke bottles with his teeth. He acted really tough and also had the ugliest, meanest look-ing dog Amber had ever laid eyes on.

The most interesting thing about Pig was that he was a Catholic and the only one the kids had ever seen up close. He wore a medal on a chain around his neck and so did his dog, Rebel. These medals protected them from everything, even lightning striking, Pig had told Amber privately. He had taught her a prayer to say whenever she heard an ambulance siren to help people that were hurt or dying. This was a very secret Catholic prayer and usually only honest-to-goodness Catholics knew all the words. She was so grateful to Pig she gave him her glass paper weight with a model head of George Washington inside. It was full of water and snow-flakes fluttered down on his head and shoulders when you shook it. Joel said he thought it looked as though old George had a sensational case of dan-druff, but it was still one of Amber's treasured possessions. Pig was crazy about it, which made Amber suspect that he just acted tough but was really nice on the inside. She hoped his Catholic dog was, too.

The white light in the ceiling hurt Amber's eyes as she leaned back in the dentist's chair. Dr. Gray's smiling face was so close she could see herself re-flected in his glasses. At last, he was through! "Heh, heh, heh," his laugh smelled strongly of Listerine mouthwash!

"There now, young lady. Your braces are tight enough for today. But you be sure and come back in two weeks and we'll work on them again. My, you were certainly a fine, brave girl. Don't you want to see yourself in the mirror?"

"No sirree, I sure don't." Amber spoke through

what felt like a barbed wire fence on her front teeth.

"Now, now, they don't look bad at all and one of these days when you're all grown up, you'll be so glad your mama had this done for you. Why, you might even grow up to be Miss Alabama, might'n you? Heh, heh!"

Amber shuddered at this idea as she struggled with the chain holding the white cloth about her neck. Ugh! There was spit and junky slimy stuff on it. Boy, if she ever had a kid, she wouldn't care if his teeth were crooked as a corkscrew. She'd never make him go to the dentist!

In the outer office, she stubbornly clamped her lips together while her mother paid the bill. Outside, they headed toward B. B. Brown's Store in silence. Finally, Mrs. Wellington said gently, "Amber, you will only need these braces for about a year. Angel, try to be a big girl and understand it's for the best." Amber almost started crying, she felt so sorry for herself. She hated to upset Mother who was always kind and good. But darn it! She could hardly talk with this fence in her mouth.

After shopping, she carried the bag that had her new ruffled dresses inside and also the red tee shirt she'd picked out for herself. It was for the official club meeting; Joel made all the guys wear something red to every meeting.

The court house clock in the square struck one o'clock as they passed by.

"Oh my gosh, I'm late," she exclaimed aloud.

"Late for what?" Mother asked, fishing in her purse for bus money.

"Oh, never mind." Amber held fast to her vow of secrecy to Joel. After all, a promise was a promise.

2

The Stolen Ham

At home, Amber quickly changed into a shirt and jeans and halted just long enough to look at her braces in the bathroom mirror. Well, they weren't too bad as long as she didn't ever smile again.

Gran was waiting at the kitchen table downstairs, still dressed in her "shop clothes," anxious to see Amber's dental work. On a half-day like Saturday, Mrs. Stone stayed dressed up when she came home in case folks came to call.

Squirming with impatience, Amber endured Gran's inspection and then rushed out the back alley and across the field. It was almost two o'clock, an hour late. What if they had started without her? Oh gosh, she'd just die.

Amber gave the secret knock. She heard loud whispering inside as the shed door slowly opened a crack. Pig saw her and grinned.

They were all in there, Pig, Tommy Lee, Joel, Little Bob and the youngest, Ecclesiastees, who was called Clee for short.

"We got somethin' for you, Wellington," Pig said. "Somethin' real good."

As she squeezed in the small shed, Amber sniffed. There was one awful smell in there. Why, it was a cigar! That devilish Joel had a real, live cigar!

They were passing it around the circle, each boy taking a deep draught.

Pig spoke again. "We're takin' time about with our puffs and you're up next." He exchanged looks with Joel who sat with his feet propped up on the wooden crate in front of him which served as a desk. He greeted her.

"Here you go, Wellington. You said you could do anything the rest of us could do, remember?" Joel handed the cigar to her. Ugh! The end of it was all wet and squishy.

Bravely, she took a puff and her stomach gave a big jump. Oh my gosh, she was going to throw up! The boys laughed as she gagged and coughed.

Amber gritted her teeth. She made a resolution she wouldn't throw up, couldn't throw up, not if she kept her jaws locked tight as a snapping turtle holding on till it thundered.

"Eewh," she gasped, "that thing's downright putrid, Joel."

Pig was still grinning through his broken teeth as he spoke.

"Well, you been frettin' to get in the Daredevil Club, Amber, ain't you? You been braggin' all week 'round here how you can do anything we do, and we got a whole mess of things lined up for your initiation."

Joel led the group out into the field, and Amber had to do handstands and jumping jack exercises followed by a long period of standing on her head, while the boys watched and shouted criticisms. Panting with fatigue, she watched Pig clear the ground for a game of "Mumeldy Peg" with Joel's brother's new jack knife.

"Okay," Joel said. "Rules are: the loser digs up these wood matches with his teeth."

"What you mean to say, Joel, is *her* teeth," said Tommy Lee, glaring at Amber. But she felt good. She'd played this game plenty of times with Uncle Tut. At last she'd show these smart alecks a thing or two.

Tommy Lee squinted at Amber in the sunlight.

"You sure do look awful with all those wires on your teeth," he snickered. "Looks just like a dog muzzle."

Amber felt her face getting red hot.

"Shut up about Wellington," snapped Joel and because he was the president of the Daredevils, Tommy Lee shut up.

They began the game in earnest. Each member flipped the shiny knife, trying to make it stand upright in the soft earth. Amber played skillfully and at the end of the game it was Ecclesiastees who knelt and rooted in the dirt with his teeth for the kitchen matches. He was embarrassed that Amber, who was a girl, had beaten him and played as well as the others.

Walking down the alley, Amber felt sorry for Clee. He was wiping his face and spitting dirt. She, too, had dreaded the idea of rooting, especially with her new braces on.

"Look here, Clee, you're only nine and since I'm a whole year ahead of you, I should be better at that old game. Don't feel bad, Clee."

But Ecclesiastees simply gave her a disgusted look and bent to tie his tennis shoes to hide his shame. Amber walked on, wondering about the really big test of courage they had planned for her.

The Daredevils were the envy of all the other neighborhood kids and their motto was "Fear Nothing." Joel had painted this sign in oxblood shoe polish all over town. Why, you could read it on the gate at the stock car racing track and even on the underside of the third pew in Brother Barker's own church, if you laid on the floor. Boy, he'd have made the congregation have silent prayer for Joel for a whole week if he had ever suspected that.

As they walked along the back alley, the delicious smell of roasting barbecued hams filled the air. Hmm-mmm. Boy hidy, that meat from the barbecue pit in back of Old Larnie's cafe sure did smell scrumptious! They clustered around the screen door of the wooden building. In the dirt floor, the huge beds of red hot coals simmered and sizzled as hot grease dripped from the rows of cooking meat.

"Dag! There must be near on to twenty hams turnin' on them spits!" breathed Little Bob over Amber's shoulder.

Large iron kettles filled with greasy scum and chunks of fat stood in the corner near a long wooden table. On it lay metal tongs and basting brushes in a big container marked "Larnie's Special Bar-B-Q Sauce."

"Gosh dog, I'm 'bout to die of hunger," murmured plump Tommy Lee, who worshipped food.

The smell of hickory wood chips smoking coupled with the tangy bite of barbeque sauce on the roasting ham made Amber's mouth water. No wonder Larnie did such a spectacular business in Bluntsville! He served the best meat in town in his cafe. Gran always said that after twenty-six years in business with his secret recipes, old Larnie must be 'bout a millionaire by now. "There warn't no flies on Old Larnie when it came to makin' a dollar" was the saying around town.

"Okay, Wellington," Joel said, waving his hand grandly toward the cook house. "There it is; there's your final test of courage."

"What'cha talking 'bout, Joel?"

"Why, you're gonna take one of those hams, that's what! And you bring it back to the shed for us to eat. Then you'll finally be a full-fledged Daredevil member."

"But Joel, are you crazy? That's stealing! If I was to get caught, Gran would kill me. Why, Clee and them didn't have to do something this bad——"

"Brave, not bad, Wellington," interrupted Pig.

"Brave? I call it just plain low-down criminal stuff. Stealin' a ham from Old Larnie? Look here, he doesn't even have the door locked."

"Yeah, that's right," said Clee. "But looky over yonder; he's sure got that old shack locked up tight." He pointed to a weathered shack next to the cook house.

"Reckon that's where he keeps all his money?" drawled Little Bob.

"Never mind that old shack. Come on, Wellington. It's now or never," said Joel. He reached inside his black leather jacket and handed her a burlap bag emblazoned with a red devil's face.

"You put it in here and we'll meet you back at the club. If you really want to be one of us, you got to do it, Wellington, and if you don't, you can just go play with those girls down the hill and never bother us again."

As the boys turned away, Pig came back. He put his St. Christopher medal around her neck. "Go on; he's not gonna miss one little ham," he said.

Joel was the last to leave. He whispered, "Fear nothing, you can do it. Go on; don't be scared," and ran down the alley.

Amber stood alone, clutching the burlap bag with sweating hands. She stared in at the smoke-filled building. Oh brother, this was the worst thing she'd ever done in her whole life. But, after she was in the club, she could always save up her allowance and pay Old Larnie back, couldn't she? Heck yes, that's what she'd do. She could just sneak back in sometime and leave money on the table with an unsigned note.

Her mind made up, she moved cautiously toward the door. Why, oh why did she wear this stupid red tee shirt? Somebody was sure to notice her in it but there didn't seem to be anybody lookin' out the back of the cafe, so here goes nothing——

Inside, the heat was terrible. Her eyes smarting, Amber neared the spattering coals. Suddenly, she spied a chunk of meat cooling on a rack. The glistening crust was deep brown, and the meat juices dripped onto the pan underneath. She tumbled the warm ham into the burlap bag with shaking hands and stepped quickly out the door.

Turning the corner, who should she meet, face to face, but Old Larnie! He fairly trembled with rage and his leathery old face was twisted into a knot as he angrily struggled to speak.

"Amber Wellington. What in tarnation you doin' f-f-foolin' around my bobby-Q? You-you got somethin' in that tote sack? You give it here this minute, girl."

Amber gasped in fear and stepped back to avoid his outstretched hand. Still clutching the bag, she swerved and ran. The old man didn't attempt to follow but stood with his hands out, shouting at her. His voice was quivering in anger.

"You-you come back here with my bobby-Q! You stop right there, you here me?"

But Amber just kept on running. Her heart pounded so that she could hardly breathe. A sick feeling crept over her as she headed across the field to the club house.

"He saw me! He saw me! He knows it was me!" she chanted out loud to herself as she ran. At last she was there and she shoved and kicked at the shed door. Never mind the secret knock now. Inside was Joel and safety. She had to get in for her heart was close to bursting!

Slamming the door behind her, she stared wild eyed around the small room. It was empty! Empty? Where were the boys? Why, those dirty, low down dogs had left her all alone, holding the bag! She looked down at the burlap bag still clenched in her hand. In a rage she threw it down on the floor, feeling exactly like a criminal.

Maybe bugs and rats would eat every bit of that stupid ham. She was going to wring Joel's neck for this when she got close enough to him. She might end up in jail for thievery.

Amber waited for a long time peering out the cracks in the shed walls to make certain Old Larnie hadn't followed her. Finally, when she thought a long enough time had elapsed, she slipped out the door and ran like greased lightning to the safety of her own house.

The Deal

Amber sat at the kitchen table eyeing her lunch. It was her favorite—pork chops, potatoes, and a dill pickle—but she just plain couldn't eat for worrying.

She watched Alta May touch her fingers to the dry laundry starch powder in the saucer, then lick each finger carefully.

"How come you eat starch when you iron, Alta May?" Amber wanted to know.

"Jes' 'cause my momma always did, I reckon, honey." Alta May looked at her. She narrowed her eyes over the steaming iron and spoke sharply.

"Girl, you got yourself into some kind of trouble

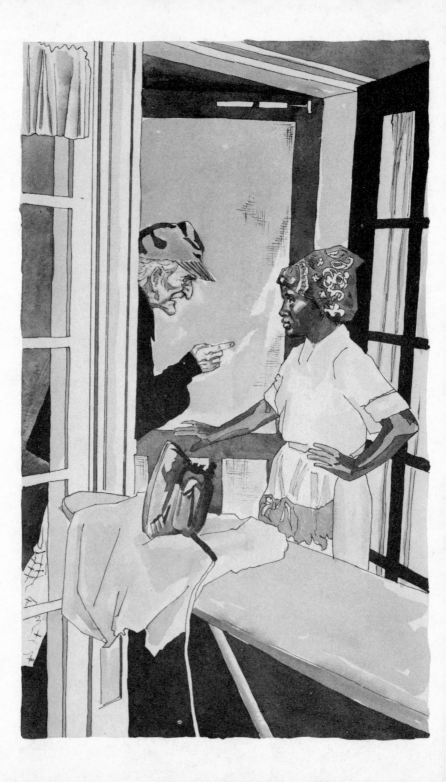

when you started stealin' from that poor old man! Your Gran's gonna skin you, if you don't put it to rights."

"But Alta May, how? I told you that Joel swore up and down to me at the lake yesterday the ham wasn't even in the club house Saturday evenin'. He said just the burlap bag was there empty! I even threatened to tell his daddy all about the club and he still stuck to his story. He was telling the pure dee old truth too, 'cause he sure doesn't want Brother Barker to know about the club. His daddy hates the devil and all his works with a purple passion."

"Sound like the devil's got ahold of you, gettin' in such as that."

Amber wriggled impatiently. She slipped the pork chops down from the plate and into her pocket so Alta would let her be excused from the table. She absolutely was not hungry. She could give the chops to Rebel later, if she was over her sick spell, that is. Pig's dog had been thrownin' up all over the place for the last two days and then eating it up again! Urp slop!

Both Amber and Alta May jumped as they heard a knock at the back door. Peeking through the side window, Amber saw a man's blue cap silhouetted against the climbing ivy. It was Old Larnie! Alta May gestured to her and Amber crouched under the kitchen table. Then the old woman opened the door.

"Hidy, Alta May. I gotta mind to talk to that little gal you keep." As Larnie turned his head aside, he spat tobacco juice. He and Alta watched it drip brownly from Mrs. Stone's prized white lilies. Her voice showed mild annoyance as she answered him.

"Aft'noon, Mister Wilkins; ain't nobody here but me. I'll be glad to send her on down to the cafe when she come back, though."

"Well, I reckon I could jest speak to Miz Stone this evenin' then. She'll be wantin' to hear what I got to say."

Alta May shook her head. "Miz Stone ain't gonna want to be bothered, Mister Wilkins. She's a busy woman. I'll jest send Amber right on down. You can settle your bizness with her, I reckon. I gotta go now, Mister Wilkins, my iron's scorchin'. Aft'noon to you."

She closed the door quickly, frowning down at Amber hiding under the kitchen table. They heard the shuffling steps on the flagstone walk and knew the old man had gone.

"I jest got one thing to say to you and that is, real ladies don't steal nothin'! Not hams, not money, not nothin'! You hear me? That Joel may have the smarts but sometimes he ain't got no more sense than a jack rabbit! Now, you get that bad little old Barker boy and get on over to the Wilkins place. You tell Mister Wilkins y'all will do some chores or somethin' for him if he'll not tell on you. And next time you 'member you're a lady! Go on, Amber, you got yourself into this here mess and you gonna get yourself out."

"Oh, Alta May, thank you, thank you." Amber said, hugging her. "I just knew you would come up with something."

She ran to Joel's house and found him in his garage, cutting a red rubber inner tube into strips.

"Hey, Wellington, I'm making all of the members some sling shots. Want one?"

"Don't act so nicey nice to me, Joel. That was one dirty trick y'all played on me Saturday, not being at the club. Like I told you yesterday, since I was the one that got caught, you're gonna have to share the blame with me. You're the president, aren't you? Well, we got to get over to the cafe right now 'cause Old Larnie's tellin' Gran tonight!"

Joel scowled. "Listen here, Amber, you know we just have your word that you ever really took the ham in the first place. I told you that when I got there that night. Now, just where is that ham, huh?"

This was more than Amber could stand. Now she was really mad. "I swear on my father's grave I took it straight to the club, Joel!"

Joel snapped the strips of rubber. "Well, anyway, all I know is, I sure do hate to do penance for a sin I hadn't even had the pleasure of tastin'!"

"Yeah, you can sure sound like a preacher's son

31

when you're tryin' to get outa something. Well, you're not gettin' out of this. I wouldn't do it to you, Joel."

But finally he agreed to go with Amber to the cafe.

As they sat talking to the old man, Larnie leaned back in his chair and whittled. From time to time he cocked an eye at the children and spat tobacco juice. It landed dangerously close to Amber's tennis shoes.

Eventually, an agreement was reached. If they would clear his back lot of all the crates and rubbish and carry it down to the city dump by the end of the next week, Old Larnie would keep his mouth shut about the theft.

"There's jest one thing, young'uns. I don't want you messin' around my tool shed. You can clean ever bit of trash up and chop them crates into kindlin' but you keep outer my private property, you hear? I'm gonna be watchin' from out the back. Now you git on to work. You jest plain lucky I didn't call the law on you!"

Larnie rose to his feet and shuffled inside, banging the door behind him.

For the next three days, all of the Daredevils worked hard. They chopped orange crates into wooden sticks and tied them in neat bundles. They loaded boxes and rusty cans into wagons, tying the handles onto the backs of their bikes and hauled them to the dump. Joel and Pig found metal scraps and wire that they saved for club use while Little Bob stood around, doing as little as possible, limping on his famous trick knee.

Tommy Lee complained loudly every day about Amber's getting caught. "That's just what'cha get when you let a girl in a club," he said for the third time, within Amber's earshot. Tommy was pulling mightily on a rusted car jack wedged between the cook house and Larnie's tool shack.

"Hey, look out, Rebel," he yelled at Pig's dog. "Rebel's got ahold of somethin', y'all. Looky here, she's got a baby rabbit."

They all stopped their work and ran to see. Sure enough, there was a furry brown rabbit. When Pig shook it loose from Rebel's jaws, it stood frozen in fear for a moment then scurried under a loose board of the shack. Rebel sniffed frantically and began to dig in the soft ground under the board.

"I bet there's a whole mess of rabbits in there. We could each of us have one," said Clee excitedly.

"You better get Rebel on away, Pig," Joel told him. "You know what Old Larnie said 'bout his precious tool shack." Clee was disappointed but the afternoon was almost gone, so they decided to quit work and get an early start the next morning.

As Amber walked through the gate to her own yard, she was grateful that Mother and Gran were at the shop all day. They didn't even suspect for a minute she was slaving away for Larnie and she knew Alta May wouldn't tell in a million years. Club secrets were safe with her.

That night, after her bath, she tried to lie awake and think about all the club plans for this summer. The Daredevils were having slingshot practice every day with balloons for targets since Joel said it was a sin to kill one of God's creatures. Oh, and they were going to enter the fishing contest down at the big spring. Wonder what Joel would do if he caught one of God's fish? And then they were planning to. . . .

But soon Amber was asleep.

Amber awoke to see Mrs. Stone's worried face looking down at her.

"Amber, what in creation were you dreamin' about? I never saw such an expression on a child! You know what you were doing? Grinding your teeth, that's what!"

Amber sat up in bed. "What time is it, Gran? Aren't you going to the shop?" It was Friday morning and the sun looked high in the sky already. She rolled over to look at her Big Ben clock. 10:15? The boys had been working an hour and fifteen minutes and she'd been wallowing a' bed! Hurriedly, she began to dress as Gran stripped the sheets from Amber's bed for the laundry man's pick up.

"Amber! What's that all over your back? Do you have a rash? Why, Amber, I swear I believe you've got the measles."

Amber looked down at herself in horror. Red spots swarmed on her chest. Spots everywhere. Looking in her mirror she saw her face was splotchy pink. Oh, no, not measles of all things! Why couldn't it be something easy, like poison ivy? Gloomily she sank into a chair as Gran whipped fresh sheets on the bed. She talked a blue streak as she plumped pillows.

"Now isn't that just the way? Here I stayed at home today, planning to have the carpenter up here to put new screens in all these upstairs windows and you go and get the measles!" Sympathy overcame her for a moment. "Do you feel real bad, Sniggle Fritz?" She laid her hand gently on Amber's cheek. "Didn't Carey Anne's sister just have the measles last month? And didn't I tell you to stay away from over there?"

It was true and Amber felt guilty remembering how she and Carey had jumped on the mattresses from the sick room. Carey's mother had put them in the yard to sun away the germs.

"What a way to spend summer vacation," Amber thought to herself as she climbed back in bed. Downstairs, Mrs. Stone was busily calling the doctor and the carpenter in her "business voice."

4

Old Larnie's Secret

Joel waited behind the bushes until Alta May had turned the corner. She'd be gone at least twenty minutes as she was carrying empty coke bottles and he knew that meant she was going to the store. He had to tell Amber the big news.

He tried the back screen door gently and it opened, but the wooden inside door was locked up tight. Hoping that Mrs. Wellington wouldn't be home on a Thursday, Joel knocked loudly. After a moment, Amber's face peeked out the lace curtain. Immediately, the door swung wide and Amber was grinning from ear to ear, her braces forgotten.

"Oh, Joel, good, good, good! Come on in. I've been about to die of loneliness this whole week. I've only had one visitor and that was just Carey. Alta May's gone to the st——"

"Wellington, just shut up and let me talk. Look at what I brought to show you."

From out of his leather jacket, Joel drew a velvet box. He set it on the kitchen table and motioned to her. As Amber lifted the lid she saw a small piece of dirty green paper. That was all.

"What's so great about a piece of old paper? It's a pretty jewelry box though. Is it your mother's?"

"Boy, are you dumb if you don't know what that is. Don't you have eyes in your head?" Joel clutched his hair in exasperation. She looked closer. It was a triangle of grayish green paper with a number printed on it. One hundred. Why, it was a corner off a one hundred dollar bill!

"Where'd you get it?" she whispered in awe.

"Now listen, I gotta talk fast or Alta May'll be back. Do you swear not to tell one word of this, no matter what happens? Take the club oath, quick!"

Amber raised her hands to her head, sticking each index finger up to form curved devil's horns. "The devil take me straight to hell if I betray the club or any of its members. Fear nothing." She recited the pledge rapidly.

"All right. Here's what happened. You know that rabbit we found? Well, Clee wanted one of those rabbits so terrible bad he sneaked back down to the shack that same evenin' when it was dark. I was cuttin' through the back alley and saw him over there prizin' up a loose board with a crowbar. He jumped a mile when I sneaked up on him 'cause he thought it was Old Larnie. Anyway, I helped him feel around in there. We pulled out three baby rabbits but they were dead. It looked like a cat or somethin' had chewed 'em. We did find one though and it seemed okay except for being scared. Clee had his mind dead set on keepin' the live one and takin' the dead ones home in our club's bag to give 'em a bang up fancy burial."

"Joel, you should have left it for its mother! You know perfectly well Clee's daddy never lets him keep any animal he brings home and he gives poor Clee a lickin' besides. That baby rabbit's gonna die and be on your conscience," Amber argued.

"Look here, do you want to hear what happened or don't you!"

"Oh, go on and tell it. Don't be so touchous!"

Joel continued. "Just as Clee was dumpin' the rabbits in the bag, I saw Old Larnie comin' out the back carryin' some trash. He dumped it in the bin and then he kept on comin' right toward us. We laid low behind the big oil tank outside his shack, you know? And as he got closer, he took out a whole bunch of keys. He flicked on his flashlight and it seemed to us like it took him 'bout an hour to get all those locks undone. We didn't dare to move for fear he'd see us. But get this, Wellington! When he got inside the shack we could look right in through that hole in the planks. He flashed his light all 'round the shack, and I could see it was practically empty save for a bunch of cans sittin' up on a shelf. Then Old Larnie stuck some folded-up papers down inside one of the cans. He wasn't in there but a minute.

"When he went on back to the cafe, Clee and I beat it out of there quick. Clee went on home and I'd just hit my yard when I remembered that piece of board we'd left lying loose. Next morning Larnie'd be sure to notice it. I took my hammer and two nails back with me real quick. Okay Wellington, this is the good part! When I got back over there it was pitch black dark, so I had to set Bubba's Boy Scout lantern on the ground beside me to see what I was doin'. Well, since I was right there, I got really curious to know what Old Larnie was hidin' in the gas cans. So, I used the hammer to lift the rest of the board on up and squeezed right inside the shack sideways. I could see fine with the lantern burning and you'll never guess what was in that can! You ready? Wellington, it was money! Real money! Lots and lots of little rolled-up bunches of money. I even shook some of 'em out on the floor. There was tens and twenties and hundreds and fifties. I tell you I never saw so much money in all my life! And that's not all. I lifted up those cans on the shelf and they sounded like money was in them, too. When I shook them I could hear rustlin' noises. They didn't slosh like they would with gasoline. The lids were rusted shut on most all of 'em so I only got to look in the one can. Then I just tore off this one hundred dollar bill corner and put the rest of it back. This is living proof of the money!"

"But Joel, you aren't thinking about stealing Old Larnie's money are you? Didn't we get in enough trouble about that stupid ham?" Amber was thrilled by the story, but she sure didn't want any part of a robbery.

"Steal it? Why, I could have stolen every dollar he had if I'd wanted to. But, I didn't even take one dollar! Not one dollar! I will say I had the biggest struggle with temptation you ever saw, but I left it all there. Besides, maybe he goes out and counts it from time to time. Listen, the board's all fixed but I can open it easy as pie. I already showed this one hundred dollar bill corner to Pig and Clee. And I'm plannin' to take Tommy Lee and Little Bob over there first chance I get. Can't you go? You're okay aren't you? I don't see a single measle spot on you."

"No sirree, she sure ain't okay! Not by a long shot." Alta May's voice spoke right behind them. They nearly jumped out of their skins in fright. She stood holding the grocery bag carefully so as not to rattle while she slipped up on them. Amber wondered how much of Joel's story she had heard.

"You little Barker boy, you clear outer here right now! I better not catch you 'round here till Amber's well and fittin' to play outdoors. What makes you so bad anyway?"

She turned back to Amber as Joel scooted out the door clutching his velvet box. "And you, young lady, you high tail it back to that couch and stay there!"

Obstinately, Amber lingered by the back door. She had a lot to think about. How could she stand to miss this opportunity to see thousands of dollars? Maybe it was even millions! Joel had his back to her as he walked slowly along the high rock wall surrounding Mrs. Stone's rose garden. Balancing precariously, he lifted one foot and glanced back at the house. He saw Amber looking through the glass top of the kitchen door and winked at her. Amber's heart swelled with pride. That Joel was a real daredevil all right.

Time dragged by slow as molasses running in January frost. At last the day came when Amber was allowed to play out in the back yard in the late afternoon sunlight.

She felt like a bird let out of a cage as she strolled around the yard, casually showing off her new yo-yo to the envious Pig.

"Come on, Wellington, let me have a turn. Just let me have one turn to show how I can do 'skin the cat.' It's one of the hardest things to do with a yo-yo and I'm a real expert!"

Amber ignored Pig's eager-reaching fingers.

"Where's your own yo-yo, expert?" she asked, as she looked proudly down at her brand new Butterfly yo-yo equipped with pen light batteries to shine in the dark. She twirled the glistening toy and did a perfect "round the world."

"Listen, Wellington, I'll tell you some mighty educational religious news, if you'll give me just five minutes with that there yo-yo!" Pig pleaded.

Amber looked at him for a moment and then gave him the toy. She sat on the curb and watched him as he twirled and talked. Pig told her how he had to go once a week to confess his sins to a special "Father" that ran the Catholic church in town. She was fascinated to hear Pig describe how he sat in a little telephone booth type closet with curtains on it to clean his conscience. After spouting off to the Father and getting a scolding he could rest easy for the coming week. It sounded like a good arrangement.

"I told him all 'bout us puttin' you up to stealin' the ham, too, but he won't breathe a word to anybody," Pig declared.

"Didn't he think we all were low down dirty skunks?" asked Amber.

"Well, yeah, he made me see the light 'bout being a 'akcess-or-ree to a crime' he called it and I had to say ten Hail Marys for penance. I told him 'bout Rebel, too."

"Rebel? What about Reb?" Amber wanted to know.

"Why didn't Joel tell you? She was the one that got that ham you stole. She ate the whole bloomin' thing! Why, I caught her buryin' the bone up near the back alley. She's terrible 'bout buryin' things. Once she buried one of Daddy's twenty-two ninety-five dollar boots and he threatened to set fire to her, he was so hoppin' mad! Hoppin' mad, get it?"

"Pig Brooks, you give me back my yo-yo! You mean you got the gall to tell me after all this worrisome time that your ugly old dog ate my ham? My ham that's caused me nothin' but grief? You and Joel make me sick!"

She turned to stomp inside the house. So that was why Rebel had been throwing up all over the place a while back. Why, that hoggish dog had been so chock full of stolen ham she couldn't even contain it all. Why in the world hadn't she realized herself that it was Rebel who had eaten that ham?

"But wait, Wellington, you ain't heard everythin' yet. Guess what? Good old Rebel is gonna have pups. Daddy says it's a true fact!" Pig reached down to tug on a tick lodged in Rebel's scarred ear. He patted his dog and looked up at Amber, smiling.

"How would you like ownin' a little pup of your very own, Wellington? I'll give you one, I promise," he offered.

Amber's angry expression underwent a complete change. Beaming with happiness, she knelt beside Rebel who obligingly rolled over on her back so Amber could scratch her plump tummy. "Oh Pig,

that's the most wonderful news! Imagine! Rebel's gonna be a mother. And you'll really give me one of the babies? Oh Pig! Thank you, thank you! Here, you take my yo-yo on home with you and keep it for the night. We can take turns with it. You have it one day and me the next, okay? Gosh, imagine! Real little babies, I can hardly wait!"

Later that evening, she tossed restlessly on her wrinkled bed sheets. With a jolt she sat up, tensely listening to the piercing shriek of sirens. Ambulances and police cars whined their way closer and closer.

She strained to see in the moonlight out over the low-sloping roof by her bedroom window, but without success. As the noises grew louder and louder, she realized the cars were stopping in the back alley right behind her very own house!

Impatiently, she went from window to window looking and listening. She cut off the window fan to hear better. She thought she heard a peculiar kind of whistling bird outside; what in the world?

She turned to go downstairs and find out if her mother or Gran knew what all the commotion was about when she spied a figure crouched against the white background of her graveled driveway. More whistling. There came a spattering of rocks on her window sill. Why, it was Joel creeping up, and right under Gran's nose, too.

Hurriedly, Amber unlocked the screen window and leaned far out so as to talk with him.

"Joel, Joel, what is it? What's going on? What is all that racket?" she called down in a hoarse whisper.

The boy's face glimmered palely up at her in the dim light. When he spoke, Amber stood still with the shock of the news. Stinging tears came in her eyes.

"Wellington, somethin' awful's come on us all. Poor Old Larnie's been found stone dead."

5

The Red-Headed Stranger

The clouds rained buckets outside as Joel, Pig and Carey Anne played Monopoly with Amber in her upstairs room. Carey was winning the game and Joel just couldn't stand it! As Amber rolled the dice, Pig mentioned Old Larnie for the second time that afternoon. "You think it really was a heart attack, Joel?"

"You asked me that a million times, Pig. I already showed you the newspaper clippin' where it said 'Ralph Lichty found the deceased dead apparently of heart failure' plain as could be. And I told you when Daddy went over there with the sheriff he saw Old Larnie up close, lyin' just as peaceful, right on his cot. He even had his Bible right there open where he must have been readin' and died in his sleep. Daddy was real gratified he went like that. Too bad your folks won't let you go to the funeral, Wellington. Our family never misses a funeral. My mother just eats 'em up!"

Amber wasn't listening. "My toy landed on jail but I'm just visiting," she said happily as she gave the dice to Carey.

"Wellington, you're handing Carey Anne two hundred dollars and she didn't even pass 'Go' yet! No wonder Carey's ahead of me."

"Hey, it's three-thirty y'all; I gotta go home," Carey said. "Come on, Joel, let go of the box. It's my Monopoly set!"

Carey gathered the colored play money into stacks as Joel irritably shot paper wads at her.

"I'll see you, Amber," she called as she went downstairs. Alta May was waxing the steps and patiently wiped them again after Carey.

"I've got a Monopoly board and pieces, but the money's all been lost," Amber told the boys.

"Just think, we could play with real money if we wanted to," said Pig. "Wouldn't that be wild?"

Joel and Amber looked at each other. Why, even to think of taking Old Larnie's money out of the tool shack was a wicked idea!

"What did you keep on bringin' Larnie's name up for when Carey was here?" Joel demanded. "She might have suspected something fishy, Pig. You got a big mouth, you know that?"

Pig was silent as he fingered the St. Christopher medal on the chain around his freckled neck. Joel thoughtfully looked at Amber again. "But I will say for once, Pig, you sure got a hum dinger of an idea! It's really tempting. See, it wouldn't be like we were stealing Larnie's money. I mean if we just borrowed it for the afternoon to play with, we could put it back this evenin'. Heck, the sheriff'll probably find it pretty soon anyway and just stash it away at the court house. Wellington, wouldn't it be something to collect two hundred dollars around 'Go' and have it be real? Right in your hand?" His eyes were sparkling and Amber knew Joel was really fired up.

She argued with him. "Joel, this is just like you to want to take that money out now when it's broad daylight and Old Larnie not even cold in his grave yet! Don't you remember how you bragged to me before about how you didn't even snitch one little old dollar that first time you found it?"

Joel tried to be patient. "Wellington, you miss the point completely. Don't you see that was different? It would've been easy as pie to take a dollar or two then! And it would have been just an ordinary thing that an ordinary kid would do. This is a real test of courage. It's what you might call a grand theft. Besides, we're not gonna spend a penny for ourselves. We'll be just puttin' it to a good use for an hour or two and then returnin' it; don't you see the difference? You get it, don't you, Pig?"

Pig nodded his head at Joel but he looked doubtful.

"Okay, it's settled then. Let's tell Alta May we're gonna be in my garage making sling shots and we'll stop by the club for supplies and then ease on over to the tool shed. Nobody is gonna be out in the alley in all this rain even if it is broad daylight. C'mon y'all, let's do it. We'll come right back here."

Carrying their shoes, they tiptoed carefully down Alta May's freshly waxed steps to the front hall. Amber got out her raincoat and umbrella from the hall tree as Alta May stuck her head around the doorway. She was on her knees, waxing her way into the dining room. "What you up to?" She looked suspiciously at the boys.

Amber answered with a bald-faced lie. "We're going over to Joel's to play in his garage. See, I've got my umbrella and raincoat and everything. I'm not gonna get a drop of rain on me. Not a drop, I promise." Amber held her breath for fear Alta May would forbid her to go out.

"Did you tromp on my steps with them shoes?" Alta May looked at their feet.

"No, no, we walked just like we were on eggs," Joel grinned cheerfully as he nudged Amber toward the kitchen door. Alta May's voice followed them.

"Well, Amber, you stay out of the wet now. And you better be dry as a chip when you git back here

—by six o'clock, young lady. I got greens cookin' and your momma's gonna be wantin' to see you settin' at that table when she comes home." Alta May waxed on around the hall corner while, outside, three sets of feet pounded across the flagstone walk and out the gate.

"Shouldn't we get Clee and them to be in on it? They should be in on it, Joel." In the club house, the rain beat on the tin roof.

"We don't have time, Pig. Maybe we might have to keep the money overnight in a safe place and they could help us count it again in the morning. You take Rebel back to my garage and close her up in there. She's liable to draw attention to the shack. I swear, I've got to think of every single thing! Wellington, let's us go on, but don't bring that stupid umbrella. Hurry up! Pig, we'll meet you at Larnie's shed."

Pig slammed the club house door as he left and Joel turned to reach up for the club's devil bag that he usually kept hanging on the spike over his orange crate desk.

The bag was not there.

Joel stared unbelievingly at the rusty railroad spike.

"Joel, what's the matter?" asked Amber. Joel groaned, "Oh no, that stupid Clee!" His face turned red with anger. "That stupid Clee!" he repeated. "Wellington, I bet you he took our club bag on home with him. Or . . ." Joel paused, thinking hard. "Or worse yet, Clee mighta left it at Larnie's tool shack. I'm gonna kick him to kingdom come, if he did!"

Amber didn't understand. "But when? How come Clee had it in the first place?"

But Joel wouldn't take time to answer. He shoved open the door and the two of them dog trotted rapidly across the field. He talked to her in snatches over his shoulder.

"Remember that night with the rabbits I told you about? Clee brought our club bag on over to the tool shack to put the rabbits in. I told you 'bout it."

Amber listened, panting as she ran through the light rain. When they reached the back alley, Joel slowed down and talked through clenched teeth. He was working up a mad as he thought back on that night.

"Clee was stuffin' the dead baby rabbits in our devil bag, allowing as how he was gonna take 'em home and bury 'em. Like a goon, I took it for granted that's what he did do but knowin' what a scaredy cat he is, he just mighta got in a stew and forgot the bag when old Larnie surprised us by comin' out jingling his keys. I never once thought to check on it, either! I sure hope and pray Clee took the bag on home and had his bang-up funeral. Otherwise any fool in the world could figure out our club members had been pokin' round. That's what

52

you call 'incriminating evidence,' Wellington. It's the surefire mark of an amateur!"

"But, Joel," Amber objected, "not everybody would know the bag was ours. Hardly anybody knows much about the Daredevils and no grown-ups know at all, I don't think."

They ran on, squishing through the mud and in minutes were reunited with Pig at the tool shack.

Joel gave fresh orders. "Pig, you keep a good look out while me and Amber squeeze in here through this crack. In a minute you can come on in, too."

Joel squinted through dribbles of slackening rain in his face as he worked the screwdriver back and forth between the loosening boards. Amber squatted beside him and Pig stood in a half crouch, nervously looking around. The storm-filled sky made it unusually dark for that time of the day, and so they felt safe from prying eyes of passersby.

As the last board squeaked loose, Joel sighed with relief and slithered into the shed, motioning for Amber to be quiet and follow. Splinters ground into her wet fingers and knees as she clumsily crawled through the narrow opening. Every once in a while Amber got sick and tired of Joel's bossiness, so she sat idly picking at the splinters in her hand, half-way hoping he would gripe about that, too. She'd tell him off good and proper if he opened his mouth. Good land, she was absolutely soaked because Joel thought her yellow raincoat was too noticeable for a "grand thief" to wear, and just how could she explain that to Alta May when she got home?

Suddenly, a man's voice spoke harshly outside the shed. Why, he sounded like he was practically at her elbow! Who in the world?

"What 'cha hanging 'round this here property for, boy?" asked the voice.

In the alley, Pig stammered out a mumbled answer, while inside the shed, Amber and Joel froze in fear.

"You'd best get on home and don't come nosin' 'round here no more. You don't have no bizness here a-tall. You hear?" The man's footsteps slushed in the mud and gravel as he came nearer to Pig Brooks.

Amber heard Pig weakly muttering something about looking for his lost knife and then listened to the slip slop of Pig's tennis shoes hitting puddles at a high rate of speed, growing more and more distant. Pig had left them. They were trapped. Caught red-handed trying to steal Old Larnie's money just like slimy crooks. Lordy, Lordy, thought Amber as she sat squinched in a tight ball, her painful splinters forgotten. She kept her eyes on Joel. He showed no fear at all, just exasperation and anger. She wondered whether he had as much conscience as he sometimes let on he did. Why, she was petrified!

While she racked her brain for a reasonable explanation to make to the sheriff or whoever that man

was outside, her ears pricked up. There was a spattering on the roof and then finally a pounding of rain drops. With the sudden downpour, she heard the man's feet take rapid strides away. Joel now motioned for Amber to look and she could see a man's narrow shoulders covered by a khaki-colored shirt. In spite of the heavy rain, his orange red hair made a moving spot of color as he sprinted toward Old Larnie's cafe. He wore a uniform.

Joel grinned at Amber and she was limp with relief. Good. Thank you, rain, thank you. That man's leavin' and he doesn't even dream we're squattin' in here, us criminals, that is.

Joel's grin faded as he glanced sharply in the dim light around at the shed walls.

Joel inched his way over, searching the clammy floor for the burlap bag. There was no sign of the rabbits or the bag with the mocking devil's face on it.

"Wellington!" he suddenly hissed at her. "Look, the devil bag's not here. Thank the Lord, for once Clee did something right. He musta taken it on home with him, rabbits and all. Hey, wait a minute! The gas cans! They're every one of 'em gone. All that money's plumb vanished!"

Amber looked at the empty shelves. Only a few rusted tools lay scattered about. A shovel and rake leaned against the wall, but sure enough, there wasn't one gasoline can to be seen.

They felt carefully about the mildewed boards

and Amber shivered as disturbed spiders and other creepy crawlers scurried about. Nothing. No burlap bag. No money.

Joel was dumbfounded. He had seen the money himself only a few days ago. Could Old Larnie have moved it to the back room of the restaurant before he died? Had somebody else got ahold of it? A dozen suspicions rattled from his tongue as he and Amber carefully made their way out of the shed and over to the low hanging mimosa tree.

Suddenly he turned to her, his blue eyes afire. "The rain's slacked up! Let's check around outside the shack for the bag, and then let's sneak up real quiet-like to the window by Old Larnie's bedroom. We could at least take a look in just to see what we can see. It can't hurt, Wellington, just to look!"

Without waiting for an answer, he went out in the streamy drizzle and Amber reluctantly followed behind him. Joel was never satisfied, she thought. They still couldn't find the bag.

Joel took a few steps down the side path to look for the mysterious stranger. As Amber reached the back of the building, she recalled a sharp memory of Old Larnie when he had sat in his cane-backed chair whittling a stick and spitting tobacco juice on the fieldstone steps. Poor old dead Larnie. "It's hard to remember how mean he was to us sometimes. It's as if that doesn't really matter anymore though," she thought. She shook her head, and tried to concentrate on spying in the window without getting caught in case someone was inside. Someone like that mystery-voiced man. He might be there. Lo and behold! He was! She whispered the news to Joel and he shoved her aside to peer in.

Joel crouched like a steel spring, not taking his eyes from the red-haired figure moving about the shabby room.

"Joel, what's he doing? Let me have a chance to see, too." But Joel wouldn't budge. When the light suddenly went out in the room, he bobbed his head down below the window sill. His voice was soft but intense as he spoke.

"Amber, I wish you'd look! Our club bag is in there. It's squinched up right on this very window sill, plain as day. That man musta found it and the gas cans, too, or else Old Larnie did. Why we might have a real crime case on our hands, you know it?"

Amber was squirming with impatience, "Joel, I said what is he doing?"

Joel's head bobbed up and down, sneaking quick looks under the torn window shade.

"He's just poking in the dresser drawers and stuff. Where in creation are those gas cans with the money in 'em, I wonder?"

He was so carried away he forgot to call her by her last name, Amber noticed briefly.

Suddenly, the door knob rattled. Oh me, oh me, he's comin' outside! Amber's heart skipped a thudding kick.

They sank silently into the oozing mud on their

blue jeaned knees praying for invisibility, and luck just seemed to be with them that rainy afternoon. The unknown man rattled the knob again, apparently checking to see if it was locked, and turned back to his rummaging.

With rain dripping down their necks they watched for a few moments more. Then, they quietly slipped down the back alley to their homes, and to hot tub baths, scoldings, and fried fish with hush puppies for supper.

"Amber, has the cat got your tongue?" Mrs. Stone teased her granddaughter at the supper table. "You haven't said one word and you're just pickin' at that good food. Just think of all the little starvin' children in the world that don't have good food to eat like you have."

Glumly, Amber asked to be excused and Leah Wellington looked after her daughter with thoughtful eyes.

That night, Mrs. Wellington came into Amber's room and sat on the edge of her bed for an evening chat.

"Is something bothering you, love?" she asked Amber gently. She didn't look directly at her, but instead gave her attention to threading her needle as she prepared to hem Amber's petticoat for Sunday wear.

Amber chewed her fingernail nervously. She debated with herself silently and then decided to tell her mother. After all, there were times when a person just had to have some sound advice, weren't there?

She told her mother about the money Joel had found, that it was now all gone. Disappeared! She wondered aloud who that strange red-headed man was, the man in the uniform that was poking around in Old Larnie's stuff and orderin' folks away like he owned the place. He seemed familiar to her.

Leah Wellington listened and smiled as she glanced at Amber's face. "Honey, I might be able to shed a little light on some of your worries. This young man you and Joel saw is Leonard Wilkins. He's in the army, a soldier like your father was. He's a nephew of Old Larnie's and he arrived in town today for the funeral. You know that gossipy old cab driver, Bee Stucky? He drove him out from the train depot this very afternoon. Bee told me all about it when I came home in his cab from the shop today early. This Wilkins nephew has a perfect right to be there."

"But, Mother, where's all that money gotten to? Joel saw hundreds of dollars stashed out in the shack and now it's gone!" Amber insisted.

"Look, if it will make you feel any better, I'll give Deputy Jack Warden a call. I went to high school with him and he's an old friend. If Jackie thinks there's been money stolen, I'm sure he'll look into it. All right? I'm sure Larnie would appreciate you worrying about his belongings."

"Yes, m'am, but there's one more thing. Tonight when I was helping Gran set the table she told me she grew up with Old Larnie. Knew him all his life, and, Mother, Gran swears Old Larnie never learned to read or write, either one. Then I've been thinkin'. How come he had that Bible so neat layin' on his chest if he couldn't read? Oh, Mother, do you think somebody could have put it there after he died?"

There. It was out at last. Her most dreadful suspicion. Amber was half-way convinced somebody might have murdered poor Old Larnie and stolen his money, too. It was a terrible thought.

Her mother was shocked, Amber could tell by her face. Mrs. Wellington continued to sit there and sew and reassure Amber's fears, but she was more determined than before to call Jack Warden in the morning. She hadn't realized the child was so upset.

A Narrow Escape

"Now suppose y'all just run through this thing again for me, and, Joel, you let Amber do the talkin' this time." Deputy Jack Warden leaned back on Gran's green velvet love seat, sucking on his briar pipe. Amber and Joel sat cross legged on the shining hardwood floor facing the two adults. As Amber told the story of Joel finding the baby rabbits and the money, Mrs. Wellington served the Deputy coffee and chess pie.

Amber repeated the same account Joel had given, carefully avoiding all mention of the Daredevil Club and the ham she had stolen. She admitted to the Deputy she hadn't actually seen all of the money herself except for the corner of the hundred dollar bill. But Joel had showed that same piece of money to Ecclesiastees Jones and Pig Brooks, too. They would vouch for him and his story.

"Whereabouts are those fellows, Joel? I 'spect I better have a little gab session with them, too." The Deputy was relighting his pipe. Amber marveled at him; that man had put away three big pieces of Mother's chess pie and had refused the fourth piece only after a moment's consideration!

Amber carefully sneaked a side look at Joel. His face was white and stiff and because he wouldn't look in her direction at all, she knew he was furious with her for squealing to her mother. She dreaded the time when they would be alone. Oh brother, he would tell her a thing or two!

Finally, Deputy Warden rose to leave. He asked Joel to go with him to the Barker house to get a look at this "famous" velvet box with the piece of money in it.

Falteringly, Joel explained how his mother had thrown the old jewelry box out in the trash. His voice trembled as he told how he'd searched everywhere but his only real proof of the money was gone. He didn't have a leg to stand on, thought Amber, filled with pity for her friend. He didn't even talk like himself. Why, he looked just like a sick cat, Joel did.

Mrs. Wellington showed the Deputy to the door and Amber listened to them talking on the front porch. From behind the venetian blinds Amber watched Joel walk to the police car, not looking back.

"I wouldn't worry 'bout it, Leah," Deputy Jack said, smiling. "You know how kids are. Old Larnie may have had a few dollars stashed away and then Joel mighta just exaggerated a bit. I understand one of Larnie's kinfolk's in town? Well, he's already got ahold of any loose cash more'n likely. I'll check into it and let you know. You tell your little gal to keep away from over there though."

"Thank you, Jackie. Amber's been pretty upset over this whole thing. She's got such an imagination!"

The Deputy said good-bye and emptied his pipe ashes down on Mrs. Stone's beloved white caladiums growing in the stone urn on the porch.

Joel sat slumped and pale in the front seat of the police car, looking every inch a prisoner as they drove away.

"Amber, tell me about the missing money again! Just tell me one more time," begged Carey Anne.

The two girls were walking down Forest Avenue and Amber stopped suddenly. From the corner of her eye she noticed a man with a hat pulled low on his forehead, leaning against the lamp post. For a moment, he looked familiar. Hadn't she seen him before? The man glanced at her but quickly turned aside.

She spoke impatiently to her friend, "I don't want to even think about it anymore, Carey. That money's brought me nothin' but trouble! Nobody believes me and . . . oh, never mind! Any way, I'm sick of the whole subject. This is where I go to Sunday School."

"Gosh! It's big. What kind is it again?" Carey was looking up at the tall steeple of the old church.

"I told you a million times I'm Episcopal! This church here was built back before the Civil War. Want to see the inside? It's really something! The top part of the ceiling is built just like the bottom of a big boat turned upside down. The men in those old fashioned days just mostly knew how to build big ships and so that's how they went on and built the churches, too. Come on, we can go in; it's never locked on Friday afternoons. The Junior choir usually practices then."

They stepped into the cool interior. As the heavy oak door closed softly, the traffic noises from the street were blotted out. To Amber's surprise, the choir stalls were empty. Inside the dimly lit chapel the two girls walked soundlessly on thick carpet, admiring the stained glass windows. People said they were worth a fortune! Amber felt proud to be showing off her beautiful church to Carey. She explained about the baptismal font and, curious to see if there would be wine in the communion chalice up on the altar, she peeked in it. It was empty.

"You better get away from there, Amber! Don't

you know it's a sin to go up by the cross?"

Carey looked nervously around. It was getting dark. "We better be gettin' on home. It's a long ways to walk from downtown. Mamaw's gonna really be mad at me," she said and Amber nodded understandingly. Carey's folks were really strict and, oh brother, if she got out of line just once in a while, her daddy would get out his belt and give her a whipping she wouldn't forget.

They reached the ornately-carved doors and tugged on them, but they wouldn't budge. What in the world? They pulled harder and pushed but the doors stood firm. O Lordy, Lordy, they were locked in the church! Frightened, Amber raced down the aisle to check the other doors. Yes, the little one by the bell tower steps was locked, too, and even the side door was locked up tighter than a tick. Maybe the sexton was still on the grounds. He must have walked around locking up while they nosed about inside. Oh, maybe somebody passing by on the street would hear them if they hollered. "Carey, start yelling. Holler help as loud as you can. H E L P ! H E L P ! H E L P !"

The girls shouted themselves hoarse but nobody came. The huge church seemed ominously quiet with its thick walls and plush carpets.

Oh, wait a minute! The face of the man that was lounging around at the street corner outside flashed in her memory. Why, she knew who he was. She just hadn't recognized him without his army uni-

form on and his red hair showing. It was that Leonard Wilkins, Larnie's nephew. What was he doin'
'round here? He couldn't be following her, could
he? Surely he wasn't mad 'cause she and Joel told
the Deputy about the money, was he? Amber's
heart began to beat faster. Oh, horrors, he couldn't
possibly be in the church right this very minute? In
there with them? She began to look rapidly around
in the darkened corners of the chapel.

Without explaining why to Carey, Amber insisted she walk up and down every row of pews
while she stood by the window, ready to break it to
escape, stained glass or no stained glass. Surely that
Leonard hadn't locked them in. Why would he?
Because she'd tattled to the Deputy?

Later, satisfied they were alone, Amber's
thoughts turned back to the problem of getting out
of there. "I know! Let's get one of those poles and
unfasten the top part of a window. It's too high up
to climb out of but we can throw a message out. It
might fall over the iron fence onto the sidewalk,"
Amber said excitedly. They tore back pages from a
hymnal and found pencils by the suggestion box.
They wrote 'Help, we are locked inside this church'
and signed their names. They stuck the notes inside
their shoes and tossed them up and over the open
window but it slanted at an angle and would open
only partially. The shoes fell, plop! They landed
unnoticed in the boxwood shrubbery by the wall of
the church. Darn! Now what? "Oh, I know what,

Carey. We'll bang real loud on the organ! That'll draw attention. Come on."

They hurried to the enormous electric organ by the choir stalls but, heck fire, it was locked up, too, tight as a drum! Everything in this whole blasted place was locked, even the bells couldn't be gotten to. Boy, for a church, somebody sure didn't trust somebody!

Carey's eyes filled with tears. "I sure don't want to spend my whole night in your old 'piscopal church, Amber! Shoot, we might even have to stay all of Saturday, too! By Sunday mornin' they might find us 'bout dead of starvation." She began to cry in earnest.

Hope suddenly shone in Amber's eyes. Of course! Why hadn't she thought of the logical solution? If Joel had been here, he would have known right off what to do.

"Carey Anne, come on. We'll be out in no time." She was smiling.

"What'cha gonna do now?" asked Carey, hopefully.

"Why, I'm gonna pray, that's what! We're in a church, aren't we? Let's just go on up to the altar rail. God'll help us get right out if we ask Him."

Confidently, she knelt on the velvet cushions and prayed aloud so Carey would get the benefit of it, too. Carey knelt in the first pew timidly and listened. Amber thought to herself, "Maybe there'll be a miracle. Folks are always talking about God working in miracle ways, aren't they?" Just to be on the safe side, Amber crossed her fingers, too. It was really dark in the big church now and in the dimness she strained to see. As she prayed again fervently for help, Amber felt her stomach rumble with hunger. She bet Alta had cooked fried chicken tonight and it was long past supper time.

She wasn't sure how long it took for a prayer to get answered, so she tried to wait a fairly respectable time. Then she rose to her feet.

The girls went over to wait for the miracle to happen by the locked doors. "The blind shall see" it says in the Bible and that was the exact truth, Amber thought. She noticed for the first time that up on the top of the doors there was a latch. She never even saw it the first time, she was so scared. Well, it was as simple as pie to use one of those long window opening poles to lift up the latch and the girls were scot free. After they found their shoes and got to walking, they thanked their lucky stars all the way home. Carey was terribly impressed by Amber's praying capabilities.

Deputy Warden's car was flashing lights in front of the house and the police radio was squawking up a storm. Gran was standing out front with a policeman. Boy hidy, was she mad! She rushed out and hugged Amber, then she sent her to bed upstairs without supper. Mrs. Wellington looked like she was about to cry. She brought up Amber a sandwich and gave her a long serious talk on behavior.

It was embarrassing that Deputy Jack had bothered the neighbors and poor bereaved Leonard Wilkins about Amber again! First, he had asked him about some wild tale concerning missing money and then about Amber being missing! The only nice thing Leonard Wilkins had from their family was the boiled custard old Mrs. Stone had sent over to him in his grief earlier in the evening.

Amber was so thankful she had escaped from the locked church because tomorrow was a big day. She and Joel were going on a church camp retreat for the weekend with Brother Barker's parish. Camp Hopedale, hello. Bluntsville, good-bye!

7

Leonard Wilkins Comes to Call

At Camp Hopedale, it was 6:00 on Sunday morning. Amber came out of the girl's dormitory. "Wellington, meet me at the mess hall. I got news." Joel's voice whispered to her from the bushes. She rubbed her eyes sleepily and gave the secret "yes" sign to him that a non-Daredevil person wouldn't even notice.

Amber hoped their mothers were good and satisfied. Both Mrs. Barker and Leah Wellington had felt it was time for a 'change of scenery,' as they called it, to keep her and Joel out of neighborhood mischief. Well, now that she'd been on this church camp retreat for a day and a night, she was ready to go home. Her poison ivy rash itched like crazy. Darn! It would take her a good week at home to get rested up. She didn't care if she never went on another hike as long as she lived! Every summer she'd let Joel talk her into this camping idea. Shoot, it would have been ten times better just to stay home for the weekend. Pig and Clee were there to play with. Clee's folks didn't believe in vacations away from home except at tobacco-harvesting time and Clee always said that was nothing but pure work, anyway.

A few minutes later, when it was the girls' turn to use the outdoor shower, Amber stood frowning in the line of giggling girls. Taking a shower naked as a jaybird with three big floppy girls a person hardly knew to speak to sure wasn't her idea of "fun at camp." She gave her place in line to a girl with hives and slipped away to meet Joel outside the mess hall.

He was standing there, munching potato chips he'd sweet talked out of the camp cook. "Wellington, read this note Bubba brought to me from town last night when he drove the station wagon up here. Pig gave it to him and Bubba said he looked like he was 'bout to cry," Joel said grimly.

"It's in the club code," Amber objected, looking at the numbers scrawled on the paper.

"Well, translate it and you'll see what it says," he ordered.

"That's stupid. How come I have to translate it

when you know perfectly well what it says?" Amber was exasperated. Glaring at him, she sat down and slowly figured it out.

The note was short and desperate. Pig's dog had been missing all Saturday. He'd already checked the Bluntsville dog pound and every other place he could think of. No Rebel. The police and the dog catcher claimed they hadn't seen his dog, so Pig was sure somebody had stolen her.

"But, why would anybody want old Rebel?" Amber wondered aloud. "She's not pretty and she sure can't hunt worth a flip. She's 'bout the ugliest lookin' dog I ever did see, even if she is goin' to be a mother."

"Rebel's not mean and ugly a bit. She's a fine dog," Joel argued as he tore open another candy bar wrapper.

"Joel, I just said she was ugly. I didn't say she was mean! I know Rebel's not mean. Hey, maybe she's gone off to have her babies. Oh, I hope, I hope!" Amber reached over to break off a bit of Joel's candy bar.

As they walked back toward the showers, Amber whispered to Joel, "Poor Pig, I guess he really thought that St. Christopher medal would protect her from every single thing. I don't see how it can, but I sure hope it does. Listen, Joel, you better go on. We're almost back to the shower stalls and you know what your daddy said yesterday about you spyin' on the girls' morning shower!"

Joel grinned at her and disappeared into the trees surrounding the camp. Amber glanced at her new birthday watch. She had some questions for Joel at their next meeting right after lunch and before the meditation hour.

"Joel, let's have a talk. I gotta get your opinion, okay?" Amber asked as he climbed up in the weeping willow tree. Around them the grounds were deserted. Everybody was dunking each other in the lake and they could hear the happy screams all the way up to the marsh where they were sitting. It was the last chance to swim before going home that afternoon.

"What's on your mind now, Wellington?" he asked. Joel was hanging upside down from the tree branch, trying to blow a huge bubble with his gum. It popped and stuck all over his forehead and hung in strings from his curly hair.

"I want to talk to you 'bout what we talked about before. You know? About Old Larnie and the Bible being put on his chest by somebody? Well, do you still think it?"

Joel flipped over and dropped to the ground. He sat leaning against the tree trunk staring at her, peeling the gum from his face.

She continued, "And what's more, those gas cans weren't filled up with money like you said!" Mother called to check on me last night, and when I asked about it, she said there wasn't anything in those cans but old recipes and some torn-up Confederate money. Larnie wasn't a real millionaire at all. Deputy Jack went over there and talked to that Leonard; then the Deputy called up Mother and told her to relax."

"Confederate money, my foot!" Joel's face was as angry pink as his bubble gum. "Just exactly who said there wasn't any real money?"

"Old Larnie's nephew said it himself. He even showed the cans to Deputy Warden and they probably laughed their heads off at us."

Joel shook his head fiercely. "You even saw the one hundred dollar bill corner yourself! Explain that away, Wellington. I'd just like to hear you try!"

Amber thought about it. "Well, it might have come off some old Confederate bill. It was dark when you went in there; you said so yourself."

"I guess I know real money when I see it!" exploded Joel. He always got furious when someone doubted him. "Listen, don't you notice something strange about all this recipe business, Wellington?"

Amber spoke slowly, "Well, it does seem like a funny place to keep them, in gas cans all locked up like that."

Joel jumped up from his spot in the shade. He fairly danced around her in his excitement. "Now you're puttin' your finger on it! Remember that day when we were in the tool shed? Leonard must have taken the gas cans and got all the real money by then 'cause the cans were all gone. And he had our

Devil bag right in Larnie's room, remember? Leonard musta got the money, I tell you!"

"Oh, Joel, we don't know that for a fact," objected Amber.

"Hear me out. You said yourself Old Larnie couldn't read a bit, didn't you? Your Gran said so, didn't she? Well, how come he had his Bible so neat on his chest anyway, dying so sudden? Even if he could read, he wouldn't just stretch out and lay something on his own chest and spread the quilt so neat, if he was fixin' to die! You thought of that by yourself. And what would he want with hundreds of recipes if he couldn't read them either? Leonard musta stuck 'em in the gas cans with the Confederate money to make it look good to the Deputy."

"Well, Joel, maybe Old Larnie could read. Maybe he learned how in his old age. And maybe some of those were his secret recipes for 'Larnie's Bar-B-Q Sauce'."

"No, no! I tell you, Wellington, there's something mighty fishy and strange goin' on! It seems to me that this Leonard Wilkins fellow is tellin' a big fat lie! For all we know, he might have murdered Old Larnie and just put that Bible on his chest to make it look natural." Joel warmed to the subject. "And listen, didn't you tell me this Leonard was hangin' around your church the day you and Carey got locked in? Why, maybe he mighta been plannin' to kidnap you and for some reason he chickened out! Why, he could——"

"Just hold your horses, Joel," she interrupted. "But, I will agree with you on one thing. He is sure a suspicious actin' kind of a fellow. Since I been thinkin' about it, I remember noticin' him and his red hair once a long time ago, back on that very first day I got in the Daredevils. He was standin' out by your mother's dogwood tree near the back alley. He kicked the daylights out of that gray and white cat that hangs around. I remember that for sure. I swear that was him. He took off his hat for a minute and I saw some red hair flashin' in the sunshine. That's right peculiar now that I think of it. Old Larnie wasn't even dead yet but I know Mother told me Leonard came in on the train just especially for Larnie's funeral. Alta May's son David was coming in that very day on his furlough and it was a big occasion for Alta. I recollect that."

Joel shook his finger in her face. "There, you see? Wellington, that Leonard fellow knows you saw him in town days early. He knows for a fact that I saw the money. Why, he was already in town but he put on a show makin' out he came after Old Larnie died 'stead of before. Don't you get it? We're real eye witnesses.' Boy hidy, you and me better watch our step. I just know he's a pure dee old killer! I can feel it in my very bones."

It was a sweltering hot afternoon, and yet as they stared at each other under the weeping willow tree, Amber felt a cold chill crawl along her neck. The bell rang for meditation hour.

"All night, all day,
  angels watching over me, my Lord.
When I lay me down to sleep,
  angels watching over me, my Lord.
Pray the Lord my soul to keep,
  angels watching over me."

Both children and adults sang at the tops of their voices. Their sunburned faces were gleaming in the blinding sun as Brother Barker's pick-up truck roared down the highway. The best part of a weekend retreat was that glorious ride back and forth from Alabama to Tennessee to Alabama again, thought Amber happily.

The wind whipped her long blonde hair into tangles. She couldn't wait to see everybody at home, especially her mother. It seemed like she'd been gone for a year instead of two days. The thought of Leonard Wilkins sparked in her thoughts but she pushed that aside. Today was a good day and she'd worry about him later. Maybe he had even left town for good by now. Shoot, every time Joel preached at her she'd get all shook up over stuff, no matter what it was. He could make something exciting and dangerous out of the slightest little thing.

She joined in the chorus singing loudly, hoping she'd get laryngitis so her voice would get that lovely husky sound just like a movie star.

"But Gran, aren't you even gonna say you're glad to see me?" Amber was perched on the end of Mrs. Stone's big four-poster bed.

"You're baked redder than a lobster!" Mrs. Stone said, staring at Amber's sunburn. Finally she relented, "Sniggle Fritz, I'm glad you're home, you know that goes without my saying. Come here and give me another kiss." The old lady gave her granddaughter a hug and asked her to bring the mirror and hair brush from the dressing table. She inspected herself critically.

"Well, I look just like death eatin' crackers this afternoon," said Mrs. Stone as she brushed her thick gray curls.

"Of all the days to be laid up in bed with a pain in my side, this is certainly the worst one. I wanted to be up and about for Sunday dinner. What's more, your mother's had to manage at the shop all afternoon without me."

Amber looked at the clock. She had better hurry if she wanted to catch the bus to downtown.

"Gran, are you sure Alta May is gonna be here in another hour? I don't have to go down to the shop. I can stay here with you." Amber looked questionly at Mrs. Stone as she lay back on her satin pillows with a painful grimace on her face.

"No, no. Absolutely not. I told you. There's a surprise for you at the shop and anyway your mother can't wait to see you. You'll have the rest of the evenin' to talk to me when you two get home.

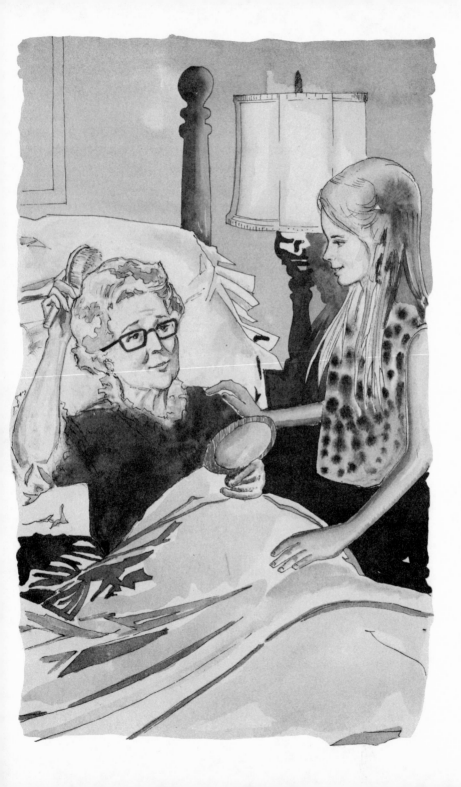

With it being Sunday, she'll close up early."

Further debate was interrupted by the clack of the heavy brass knocker at the front door. "Oh no, not company, I hope," moaned Mrs. Stone. "Amber, go see who it is and have them wait in the parlor. Then you come tell me before you show them in. Hurry now."

Amber opened the heavily paneled door and stepped back a step in shocked surprise.

The red-haired man in uniform smiled down at her. It was P.F.C. Leonard Wilkins and he had come to call.

Amber's first thought was to slam the door violently in his face but she stood hesitating. He stepped right in the doorway and spoke to her.

"So you're the little gal I've been hearin' so much about! Well, well, I'm mighty proud to meet you, Little Miss Amber. I hear you got locked up in a church on Friday. Were you scared?" His tone seemed to Amber to be friendly in a phony sort of way.

Her fears about him made her tongue-tied with shyness, and she simply gestured for him to take a seat and ran rapidly down the hall to her grandmother's back bedroom to tell her of the man's arrival.

"Who? That Wilkins boy? Well, I say! Imagine a young man like that taking the time to call on a sick neighbor! Even after all the trouble you've brought on him involving the Deputy. Amber, show him right in and you go on and catch the bus. It's due any minute. Alta May will make us some iced coffee when she gets here. Run along now, child."

Mrs. Stone reached under her pillow for her pocketbook. She dabbed on a bit of lipstick before the young man came in. "No sense greeting him lookin' like a h'ant!" she murmured aloud.

Unwillingly, Amber left them there together, alone in the big house, and as she ran for the bus she fretted, hoping Alta May would come very soon. Amber trusted that Leonard Wilkins just about as far as she could throw him.

In downtown Bluntsville, it was very near to closing time for the city stores that stayed open on a Sunday.

Amber and her mother had been busily catching up on two days of absence from each other.

To Amber's disappointment, her mother didn't seem at all concerned over Amber's excited description of the visit to Gran by Private Wilkins. She was mildly surprised but that was all. She dismissed Amber's idea that he was some sort of a villain and scolded her daughter again about her overactive imaginings.

The big surprise was a wonderful one indeed. There, parked in front of the shop, was a brand new car and it was now the proud possession of Leah Wellington. Well, the car was actually second hand but new to Amber's family, at any rate. Now they could travel in style and leisure, not having to rely on Mr. Gipson's cranky, smoking bus every hour on the hour. Amber was thrilled.

They looked up as the bell jingled on the shop door.

"Well David! I'm glad to see you," exclaimed Mrs. Wellington.

"How you doin', Miz Wellington?" asked the young man dressed in khaki. It was Alta May's tall young son. Amber greeted him, too, and looked at him curiously. He didn't look a bit like Alta. He must look like a giant beside her, she thought, Alta's so small for a grown-up.

Amber continued to sort the potpourri sachet boxes as the adults talked.

David inspected a few price tags on various items.

"Listen, Miz Wellington, I sure would like to buy Momma that hat in the window. That one with the cherries on it? Yeah, that's the one."

Mrs. Wellington brought the black straw hat over to the counter. "Oh, David, what a lovely thing to do. I know Alta May's birthday is this weekend and I'll give her some gloves and hosiery to go with it."

She wrapped the hat in tissue paper carefully as they talked.

"You know, David, every time I see someone in uniform, it makes me think of Amber's father. You remember my late husband, don't you? And we've had another young soldier in town lately, too. Wilkins is his name. Didn't you come in on the *Hum-*

mingbird a week ago on a Monday, too?"

David nodded.

"Why you might have seen or talked to him on the train. Private Wilkins? Tall fellow with red hair. He had to come in town especially for his uncle's funeral. The old man, Mr. Wilkins, was a neighbor of ours." She handed him the brightly wrapped package.

David thought as he got out his wallet to pay for the gift. "Oh yeah, I think I saw him. He's a private though, isn't he?" David looked proudly down at his own corporal stripes.

"Why yes, now that you mention it, it was P.F.C. Wilkins," Mrs. Wellington remembered.

"But he didn't come in on the *Hummingbird*, Miz Wellington. I know that for sure 'cause I noticed him sittin' there on the bench in the depot when the train pulled in, so he had to have been there before me. He was the only GI at the station besides me. If we're talking 'bout the same fellow, that is."

Mrs. Wellington paused, thinking of the gossipy cab driver telling her of picking up Old Larnie's nephew at the train station and driving him in for the funeral that day.

"Well, David, we only get the one train a day here and I was under the impression . . . Oh well, here's a little card you can sign to go in Alta's package if you want to. I just know she's going to love that hat. Amber and I will give her our gifts on Monday."

He left and Leah busied herself with another cus-

tomer. But as Amber watched her mother, she saw a frown spread over her face. She could tell that her mother was disturbed about something because that was the way her face always looked when she was worried. Amber frowned, too. Something was sticking in her mind.

All of Amber's former doubts began to nag again and she thought of her grandmother at home, sick in bed and helpless. And she had left Leonard Wilkins there in the house with her. Amber started to tell her mother about her fears but then was silent. She'd been suspicious enough for one day. Anyway, it was almost time to drive home in their very own car.

Many hours later that same Sunday night, Amber couldn't sleep. She got up for a drink of water and the voices of her Gran and mother drifted up to her. She crept over to the curved banister on the stairway landing and listened as they talked downstairs.

Leah Wellington's voice was sharper than usual.

"Mama, just what did this Wilkins boy want over here this afternoon?"

"Why, I told you at supper he was returning the bowl I sent the boiled custard over in," Gran replied.

"I mean, what did he talk about? Did he say how long he was going to stay in town or anything?"

Mrs. Stone's curiosity was aroused. "What in the world are you so persnickety about that young man

for, Leah? Why don't you just come right out and say what's on your mind?"

Leah shrugged impatiently, "I suppose it's really nothing, but all this afternoon I've been putting a few facts together in my mind and they don't seem to add up."

By now Amber was interested. She held on to the banister tightly as she listened while her mother reminded Gran of that queer story of Joel and Amber's, the tale about missing money. How Amber had insisted Leonard Wilkins had followed her in town when she and Carey were locked in the church. And just today, Alta May's son, David, had said the Wilkins boy was already in the train depot as the train pulled in.

"Well, Leah, it's just too bad you weren't home this afternoon to speculate on these matters with that boy in person," said Mrs. Stone irritably. "Why, if you had only talked to him you would see for yourself that he's a perfectly fine young man. The way he went on about his uncle's death was a sight to see. And about that money, you know Jackie Warden told you it was just old Civil War money. You know how saving the Wilkins always were."

Mrs. Wellington sighed, "Well, mama, I suppose you're right; there's probably nothing to it."

As her mother came up the stairs, Amber scurried back to bed. She threw the sheet over her face and lay there hoping her mother wouldn't suspect she was still awake. All that worrying at the shop about Gran. What a waste, she thought. Here she'd been thinking Leonard Wilkins was out to do some harm and instead he and Gran had gone outside in the back yard to slurp ice cream with Alta May. Gran sure made a miraculous recovery from that pain in her side, too, when company came to call.

Amber pretended to breathe deeply in sleep as her mother paused by her bedside.

Rebel Gets Lost

I 'm so sick of rain I could die!" Pig squeezed water out of his baseball cap. His clothes were soaked. His eyes were strained with worry and for once in his life, Richard "Pig" Brooks didn't look a bit tough. All of the Daredevil members were crouched in the club house. As the rain streamed down outside they wiped their wet faces and wearily looked at each other.

"Poor old Reb. I hope she's not out in all this wet." Pig's freckled face looked as if he might cry any minute.

The boys had been searching the neighborhood and all the houses beyond their block as far as a mile in every direction for two days calling for Rebel. The only place they had skipped was the funeral parlor and it was just for people anyway. They couldn't find hide nor hair of that dog.

Amber touched Pig's arm and spoke gently. "Pig, she mighta been taken in by somebody that doesn't even know she's yours. Why, she's probably nice and dry right now. She's in a lot better shape than us, I bet." Amber felt sorry for her friend. She looked away pretending she didn't see Pig's tear-filled eyes.

"What if she's had her pups and she's lying out somewhere sick and can't get up? What if all her pups drown! I'm goin' out and look some more." Pig angrily banged the shed door behind him as he left and the rest of them looked at each other silently. No one really wanted to go out in the rain again. It was almost lunch time and Tommy Lee said he was starved. Joel gave strict orders to meet again at the club house at 1:00 and they could continue the search. Little Bob kept giving his fake cough so everybody would understand if he didn't make it back after lunch.

One o'clock came and went and nobody showed up in the rain to search except Joel and Pig. They looked and called and whistled, and finally Joel went to Amber's house while Pig headed down town to look some more. Pig just wouldn't quit.

Joel banged on the screened kitchen door. When it opened he stood there drenched and grinning.

"Hey, Alta May, is Wellington here?"

"She's upstairs takin' a bath to get some of that mud off. Wait a minute. Stand still on that rag rug. Don't you drip all over my clean kitchen floor." Alta May's voice sounded crankier than she really felt. She threw a towel over the chair and went back to her job of peeling fresh cantaloupe at the sink. She handed Joel a slice of the juicy melon.

Amber came into the kitchen in fresh jeans and a shirt, her blonde hair hanging in wet tendrils.

"Did you shampoo that head twice?" Alta May looked at Amber suspiciously.

"Yes, yes, I did."

"Did you rinse with the lemon juice, like I told you?" Alta persisted.

"Yes, yes! Joel, you want to borrow a dry shirt from me? You look like a drowned rat. Where's Pig?"

Joel described to Alta and Amber how they had scoured the area for Rebel and not found one single clue. As he talked, he ate hot crackling bread and afterward he admired Alta May's birthday presents from Amber. There was a fancy flowered silk scarf, a half-filled bottle of "Evening in Paris" cologne and a slightly sticky oil painting of a woman. Amber had painted it herself.

"That's really good, Wellington. Who is it?" he asked, slipping one of Amber's red tee shirts on over his lean shoulders.

"Who is it? Why, it's an oil painting of Alta May,

stupid! Don't you even recognize somebody when you're right in the same room with them?"

Amber was fit to be tied, she was so insulted. She would have had more to say but there was a loud hammering and shouting at the door. It flew open and Pig practically fell in the doorway, his eyes wild with excitement. Alta May opened her mouth to scold about those terrible muddy feet but after looking at Pig's happy face she didn't say a word.

His voice was shrill with excitement. "Oh Joel! Oh Amber! I got good news! Oh boy, oh boy. I got me some good news! Rebel's at home, right this very minute!"

He danced a little jig in the puddles on the linoleum. Muddy water sprayed everywhere. Hurriedly Alta May threw a towel around his shoulders and made him sit down in the corner to talk. His breath came in heaves and gasps.

All three of them eagerly listened to his story. It seems that Rebel had her pups somewhere, Pig didn't know where, and then got hit by a car. Old Mrs. Gandolph had taken poor Rebel into her house and doctored her up, putting a splint on her leg. Mrs. Gandolph and her husband ran the funeral parlor on First Street and her place was the only one the Daredevils hadn't investigated. Everybody knew it was bad luck to go in a funeral parlor, unless you went in feet first and flat on your back, that is. Anyway, now Rebel was home safe and sound but awful weak, and Pig was so grateful to

Mrs. Gandolph he could have kissed her feet. And furthermore, if Rebel hadn't had her St. Christopher medal on, Mrs. Gandolph wouldn't have ever been able to figure out she belonged to the only Catholic family in the neighborhood. So it did protect her, after all!

The only remaining problem now was what had happened to the pups. Pig hoped they weren't dead somewhere. If only Rebel could walk, she could show him right where they were. Oh gosh, he had to get Amber and Joel and the rest of the guys to look for them. They had to be pretty close.

Amber and Joel nodded their heads rapidly in agreement. Because of poor old Reb's broken leg they'd have to find the pups without her; but they promised Pig they would look until their eyeballs hung out on their cheeks.

The two boys left in the pouring rain whooping and cutting up like warriors on a rampage, and Amber watched enviously from the back door. Sighing, she turned and began to help Alta May clean up the sopping wet kitchen floor.

Later that day they recruited help from kids on other neighboring streets, promising a reward of fifty jaw-breakers, a slingshot and one free puppy to anyone who found Rebel's litter. But it was no good. Nobody found them. When the cloudy sky finally cleared a bit, some of the bigger kids suggested a neighborhood play out after supper. They could form into teams, searching out the other teams in the dark and continue to keep an eye out for the puppies at the same time.

Everybody was satisfied but Joel who had to go to a revival night special prayer meeting with his brothers. He was mad enough to chew nails but his daddy stood guard as the family piled into the old station wagon. Amber watched them go, wishing Joel could have stayed home for the play out, too. Now she'd be stuck with Clee, the youngest kid in the gang, and he always got scared in the dark and gave himself up. She hadn't ever seen it fail.

It was getting dark outside. The bushes trembled with water drops from the recent thundershower, but at least the rain had let up long enough for them to enjoy playing outside.

She tapped her foot impatiently. Oh good, there was Clee coming now. They ran together to find a good hiding place.

"Amber, reckon Mr. Washburn will care if we hide in his old car?," Clee asked worriedly. On a neighborhood play out, they could hide from the other teams anywhere at all on their own block.

"Oh come on, Clee. Nobody will ever find us in here." She opened the door of the rusty Packard. It had been sitting back of Washburn's filling station as long as Amber could remember. Even the back car window was smashed to smithereens. As she stepped inside, something squirmed under her bare foot. Ugh, was it a snake? She heard whimpering noises and strained to see in the dark.

"Oooh, Clee! It's a puppy! A baby puppy! And here's another one. Clee, I just bet my life these are Reb's pups."

They fumbled in the dark for the soft bodies.

"How many are there?" asked Clee, holding two pups in his arms. He was simply delighted!

"Here's four more, Oh look, this one is all cold and stiff and here's another one dead. Oh Clee, two of 'em died! Didn't y'all look in this old car when you were searching?"

Clee thought for a moment, "Well, Joel assigned Washburn's place to Little Bob and he swore he searched it good and proper."

Amber snorted. "Little Bob! Why Joel ought to know you can't count on Little Bob to do a lick of work. He's the laziest boy I ever laid eyes on. He must not have even come over here to look or else he would have seen Rebel's pups easy as pie here in the car. I'm gonna vote to kick Little Bob smack out of the Daredevils the next meeting."

Clee nodded his head in complete agreement as he stroked a pup's velvety ear.

"Listen, Clee, let's take them on back to Pig's house. Can you carry three?" Amber just couldn't wait to see Pig's surprised face.

Clee shook his head. "Not without mashing 'em. We gotta get a box or somethin'. Hey, let's go back

to Joel's. He's got some orange crates in his garage and nobody's home; they're all of them gone to church. We can hurry right back."

They put the crying puppies down gently and closed the car door. They ran lickety split for the Barker's place and were forced to sit down just for a moment to catch their breaths before starting back.

"It's really dark! What'cha doin' now?" Clee was standing in Joel's yard while Amber stuck a piece of paper in the Barker's screened porch door.

"I'm leaving a note for Joel, Clee. He'll read it when he gets back from church," she explained. "He'll feel bad if he's left out of this big news. He always tells us stuff, doesn't he?"

They hurried back past Old Larnie's cook house going in the direction of Washburn's filling station. Suddenly, a figure stepped out of the shadows. It was Leonard Wilkins and he stood squarely in their path.

The Daredevils Triumph

Where you goin' with that there box?" Leonard demanded. "What'cha got in it, anyways?"

"We-we know where there's some p-p-puppies and we're just goin' to get 'em over at the f-f-fillin' station," Amber stammered. She was nervous at this unexpected meeting with Old Larnie's nephew.

"We was just cuttin' through your yard to save time. We wasn't gonna bother nothin' of yours, honest!" Clee spoke up bravely but he stepped back a few paces behind Amber.

Leonard leaned closer to look into the empty box.

"Are they real little? The pups?" he asked. "Why, they'll fall right outa them slats. I tell you what; you come on up by the back door of the cafe and I'll give you some straw to stick in there. That'll be better, won't it?"

Amber looked at him closely. Why, he was smiling! He seemed to be right friendly. She might have misjudged him this whole time.

Leonard put his hands on their shoulders and steered them to the back door of Larnie's cafe, chatting as they walked. Once there, Amber hesitated and then stepped inside the doorway, Clee close behind her. They listened to Leonard talk as he unlocked a storeroom door and pulled out a big bundle of straw wrapped tightly in wire. He cut the wire with pliers and stood holding the shiny loop of steel in his hands, slowly twisting it.

"Now, Little Miss Amber. I'm mighty curious about all this here money you been tellin' the Deputy such tall tales about. Just where do you s'pose all those thousands of dollars could be, do you reckon? Or maybe you know somethin' 'bout it, boy?" He looked sharply at Clee.

"I don't know nothin' 'bout the money," Clee exclaimed.

Amber chimed in, "That's right! That's right! Anyway, Deputy Warden said it was just old Confederate money. You even showed it to him yourself. Joel's the only one of us who saw the real ——" She stopped. Oh darn! Amber could have bitten off her tongue! Why did she even bring Joel's name up? She turned quickly toward the door, stumbling over the box half filled with straw.

"Oh no, you don't." Leonard reached a long arm over her head and held the door fast. He pulled her away, banged it shut and locked it. His voice was suddenly harsh.

"This makes the second time I've had to lock you up! I'd have gotten you straightened out even more that day in the church if you hadn't had that other snivelin' gal hangin' on your coattails!"

So! Amber realized she had been right, after all. Leonard was the one who had locked up her and Carey in the church. He wanted to scare the daylights out of her for squealing to the Deputy about that money being missing. Thank goodness Carey had been with her and Leonard had had second thoughts about threatening them together. Why, he had just been biding his time all this while!

Leonard said, "You see this here key? Well, you can have it to open that door soon as you tell me what you and them boys done with my money! Now, I know y'all got it 'cause you told the Deputy you had it right in your very hands!"

"Joel's the one that had it, not us," said Clee. Amber could tell he was really scared. She pinched his arm to make him shut up.

"Then you saw the money, too? You know about some real money?" Amber asked Leonard as she moved a bit closer to Clee.

He jerked Amber to the window overlooking the back lot as he angrily pointed and said, "I took it outer them gas cans and buried it myself, right out there in a burlap bag I found, and the hole's all dug up! Sure as I'm standin' here, y'all know 'zactly where it is this very minute. Now start talkin'!"

Leonard stood with his arms folded, high color mounting in his freckled cheeks until they seemed the same flaming red as his hair. He was really mad. He still gripped the coil of wire in his fist.

Amber stood petrified with fear at the window, glancing first out at the darkened lot then at Leonard. The tall man spat disgustedly on the floor and began to pace about the small room in silence, his forehead wrinkled as he thought.

As Amber stood staring fixedly out the window, she jumped in surprise. Joel's face was looking in at her! Right in the very same window underneath the torn window shade. She glanced quickly at Leonard Wilkins but he was leaning against the wall glaring at the floor. His back was to the window for the moment. Good! Amber silently pointed to Leonard and then drew her finger quickly across her own throat, pantomiming disaster to Joel. She rolled her eyes in alarm to show Joel their predicament and gestured wildly for him to go away. Joel nodded and his face disappeared from view. Oh, he's gone for help, thank goodness! Amber melted in relief onto Larnie's iron cot that stood by the door. Remembering suddenly that it had been Old Larnie's death bed, she sprang up again, causing the red-haired man to whirl suspiciously.

"What you up to, girl? You got somethin' to tell me?" Amber didn't answer. She glanced at Clee and saw that he was terrified, too. He was crying silently and looked as if he might faint. His eyes were huge with fear. He had suddenly noticed the curved handle of a hunting knife protruding from Leonard's back pants pocket. Clee had a horror of knives.

Amber threw her arm around Clee and spoke impulsively. "I'll get you that money! Just don't bother Clee. He's only nine years old and anyway he doesn't even know where it is. I know all about it and Joel Barker knows about what you did to Old Larnie, too!" She was blurting out the words, saying anything that came to her mind just so he wouldn't murder Clee. And if he thought she had the money, he sure wouldn't murder her either, would he? He might be afraid if she threatened him back. Leonard's lips parted, whether to sneer or speak, Amber never found out because they were interrupted by a loud knocking at the door.

Leonard wavered. He looked at the two of them and then at the locked door. Joel's voice rang out loud and clear. "Wellington? Clee? I know y'all are in there with Wilkins. Better let me in, I got some mighty important information 'bout that missing money!"

As Leonard unlocked the door, Amber thought about screaming her lungs out, but what's the use?

Her high hopes for rescue went down. Now Joel would be a prisoner, same as they were. If only she hadn't left that note about the pups on Barker's screen door, at least Joel would have lived to tell their story. He wouldn't have come looking for them and stumbled into this awful hornet's nest. Now, they'd probably all three of them end up in weighted sacks in the Tennessee River. Oh me, oh me! This was the end of Amber Wellington, age ten years. She was shocked, too. Why in the world had Joel come on in here? Oh, why didn't he go and get the police or somebody?

As Joel came in the room she saw that he had his haughty "Cyrano de Bergerac" expression on his face. The only thing he was missing was the great big nose and the French sword, of course. They had seen that movie about eight times. Joel just adored that character! Now he had his chance to be a big hero and on a church night, too!

His proud expression changed when Leonard grabbed him by the front of his shirt and slammed him against the door. "I been foolin' 'round with y'all long enough!" Leonard hissed at him. "Now you tell me what you done with that sackful of my money. It's mine free and clear and I mean to have it!"

Joel glanced over at Amber before he answered. "Well, if it's legally yours, then why'd you have to kill Old Larnie for it? We got proof you murdered him. "She," he pointed to Amber, "is a real eye witness to you being here pokin' 'round town before Larnie was even dead! And anyways, I was looking in the window when you did it. I saw you put that pillow on his face and smother him!"

Leonard released his grasp on Joel's shirt in surprise. "You loony? Murder? I never laid a hand on the old buzzard! He just keeled over out of the blue while's I was clear 'cross the room. You didn't see nobody smother nobody, boy!"

Joel was skeptical. "Yeah, that's what you say. And you tried to fix it up, didn't you? Layin' that Bible on his chest! Well, Mr. Murderer, you made the 'fatal error' they're always talking 'bout in mystery books. You know that? And I'll just tell you what it was. Old Larnie couldn't read! He even had to memorize his own secret recipes by heart 'cause he just plain could not read! So you must have fixed him up to look so fake and peaceful with that Bible plopped down on his chest. Now, you just put that in your pipe and smoke it!"

Wilkins was startled. His mouth hung open in surprise as he looked down at the boy. Joel's eyes fairly blazed with triumph. He was doing it at last! Facing real danger and not even turning a hair. He looked proud as punch!

Boy hidy, Amber had to hand it to Joel. He wasn't a bit afraid; least he sure wasn't lettin' on, if he was. She stood with her arm over Clee's shoulders, her thoughts flickering between admiration for Joel and terror for Leonard Wilkins. She couldn't take her eyes from that wire stretched between Wilkin's nervously twitching hands.

"Now, just hold on here a minute. Let's just get this all straightened out." Leonard had apparently regained his composure and he shoved Joel and Clee over onto Larnie's cot. Amber sat down, too.

"Now you kids looka here. I come down here to see my old uncle 'bout some bizness. Everybody in my family knowed he squeezed his dollars, and with me bein' his closest livin' kin and him gettin' along in years, I wanted to see was they anythin' he would give to me, bein' fresh out of service and all. But the old tight wad had sooner die than give me a penny. When it ended up with him kickin' the bucket like he did, I will admit I tried to make it look like I come in town on the train for the funeral so's not to have to answer a bunch of curious questions 'bout the old man dyin' so sudden like.

"And anyways, I got a legal right to that money and you sure ain't! Why, you could get arrested yourselves for stealin' it. They'd take you away from your mommas and put you in a special prison they got for juvenile crooks and never let you out again. But I'll tell you what. If you hand it back, I'll give you each one fifty dollars for spendin' money and I won't tell a soul 'bout you stealin' it. Now, where in the devil is that sack of money I buried?" He snapped the steel wire threateningly but kept his distance.

Joel spoke softly. He was smiling. "Speakin' of

the devil, it's a funny thing you didn't notice the devil on that bag you used. I painted the devil's face on it myself for our Daredevil Club. We been usin' that same old bag for everythin' we do, includin' stealin' one of Old Larnie's hams one time. Why, Clee accidentally left that very sack in the tool shed and you just obligingly went and used it, too. And don't deny it, 'cause Wellington and me spied on you and saw our devil bag smushed up against the window sill in this very room. So you had our bag and we know it for a fact."

"Get to the point, boy!" Leonard's voice was loud and hateful.

Joel continued calmly. "Well, Wilkins, you prob'ly won't believe this but a dog is the one that dug up that bag with the money inside. It wasn't any of us. It was just a dog."

"You're a slippery-tongue liar! Where's that there money?" Leonard's face was getting redder and more speckled. As he took a few steps closer to Joel, the boy stood up to meet him talking fast. "That's right, Wilkins. A hungry old dog smelt ham smell on that greasy burlap bag and dug it up and dragged it, money and all, to have her puppies on, and that's the gospel truth!"

His face filled with rage, Leonard raised his arms high above Joel's head. Amber stiffened in panic as she saw the glittering steel wire taut in the man's trembling hands. Lordy, Lordy, he was going to strangle Joel any minute in his lathered up state of mind!

Joel saw what was happening, too, but he talked faster and faster, keeping his eyes glued on Leonard's face. "Now 'fore you do anything you gonna be sorry for, you answer me this. How come you had to go and bury money that's legally yours anyway? Your story doesn't hold water, Wilkins."

Leonard was practically snarling when he answered, "I buried that money 'cause certain overly curious little brats like y'all tattled to the Deputy 'bout them missin' gas cans. That's how come! Why, I had to have a safe place to put it so's that nosey sheriff wouldn't hold the money up in court for some humongous long legal time like they do every time some rich old man dies. Now, you satisfied?"

Joel sneered. "Not a bit! It sounds fishy to me. I'm gonna testify in court you killed Old Larnie and stole his money, too, unless you turn us loose."

Leonard couldn't control his temper any longer. "You ain't gonna do no such thing! I'm gonna git you now, boy! I'm gonna make that old man's death look like a picnic compared to yours!"

But that was as far as Leonard got in this threat. Car wheels crunched in the gravel driveway and Amber could see a flashing blue light outside the window. It was Deputy Jack Warden, here to save them at last. Thank heavens! She and Clee collapsed into each other's arms and burst into tears.

Joel got the supreme satisfaction of giving Leonard Wilkins a swift kick in the stomach and he doubled over in astonished pain.

Amber, Clee and Joel sat huddled in the police car, still trembling from the awful experience they had just had. All the bravery had washed from Joel's expression and he looked drawn and tired. They conversed in low tones and Clee still snuffled a quiet sob, wiping his nose on his sleeve. Policemen swarmed about Old Larnie's cafe.

"But Joel, did you really see all that?" Amber wanted to know. "See him smother Old Larnie with a pillow?"

Joel shook his head. "Heck no. But I de-deuced it, Wellington, and I still betcha I hit the nail on the head, too. I betcha one million dollars he'll end up confessin' it in court. Don't you bet he will? Why, he's over there blubberin' something to the Deputy right now." Joel was convinced, all right.

"He sure looked like a murderin' son of a gun," agreed Clee. " 'Specially when he reached out them great old big hands." He shivered at the thought.

Amber had more questions. "But Joel, how come you ended up at the cafe, anyway? You slip off from church early? You get my note? Were you de-ducing 'bout Rebel and the money in the bag, too, or was that for real?"

Joel held up both hands to shush her. "Hold your potatoes, Wellington. One thing at a time. This is what happened. It's a revival night at the church tonight and with all that hootin' and hollerin' goin' on, I just eased out the side door and Daddy never missed me. I stopped at your place but they said you were out on the play out, so I went on home to get out of my good suit pants. I saw your note 'bout Rebel's pups bein' at Washburn's and I high tailed it up to Pig's house, figurin' that's where you would be, too. You weren't, so Pig hustled back with me to Washburn's and we got the pups out ourselves. That's when we found the money! Old Reb had dragged our very own devil bag full of money to the car. Money was spread all 'round on the seat and floor. Some of it was chewed up and piddled on but thousands of dollars was there all right. Me and Pig couldn't figure out where in the dickens you and Clee had got to, so we just put our heads together. We cut through Old Larnie's yard to go back toward my house, trying to figure which path you and Clee would have taken, and just naturally I had to look in the crack of light coming from under the shade of the cafe window. And lo and behold, there you were, you and Clee."

Amber said, "That's when I saw you."

Joel nodded his head. "Right. So I sent Pig on with the pups and the money to call the Deputy while I stayed to keep Leonard from killin' off you and Clee 'til help could arrive."

Joel had a very satisfied look on his face and for once Amber didn't mind. He really had saved their

lives. She looked up through the Deputy's car window at the sight of handcuffed Leonard Wilkins being taken to a waiting police car.

At last, Amber was in the safety of her own bedroom. She sipped a cup of hot chocolate as she sat propped up on her pillows. Her mother and grandmother sat in the room, observing her with worried expressions on their faces.

Mrs. Stone said, "And butter wouldn't have melted in his mouth! That Wilkins boy surely fooled me. And Amber, you mean to tell me that he was responsible for Old Larnie's death, too?"

Amber shrugged her shoulders. "Well, Gran, all I know is he told us and admitted to Deputy Jack, too, that he was in the room with Old Larnie when he died. But he swears he never laid a hand on him. He swears he really did just collapse and die and that all he did was lay him out on the cot. Least that's what he says."

Mrs. Stone sniffed, "Well, it certainly sounds to me like that Leonard really did murder his very own uncle. Poor Old Larnie."

Leah Wellington spoke. "Well, mama, it will be up to Deputy Jack to get the facts. He told me he thought there would have to be an autopsy performed. That man has certainly proved his horrible character the way he treated Amber and the other children. The most astonishing thing to me is that one of Deputy Jack's men did some investigating and found out this Leonard Wilkins wasn't Larnie's nephew at all! Apparently, while in the service he had made friends with the real Leonard Wilkins who was later killed in action. This boy, whoever he is, was just pretending to be a relative to get his hands on some easy money."

"Why that no count scoundrel!" Mrs. Stone exclaimed. "And he almost got away with it, too."

Amber said excitedly, "Yes'm, and if Rebel hadn't dug up that burlap bag with the ham grease smell on it, Leonard or whatever his name is would have stolen all that money."

"Why, it's enough to turn a person's hair snow white!" said Mrs. Stone. She slapped her hands on her knees and rocked violently back and forth in her rocking chair.

After a few minutes, she and Leah Wellington rose and each kissed Amber lightly on her cheek. As they left the room, Amber's mother brushed away her quick tears of relief that her daughter was safe.

When they went downstairs, Amber promptly snapped on the bedside lamp again. She wanted to sleep with the light on for this one night, even if it was babyish. But, gosh dog, she couldn't sleep. Her brain was buzzin' like a horse fly! "Well," she thought, "I'll be famous! Joel will be famous and all the club members, too. Why, our photographs will be splashed all over the Bluntsville *Times* newspaper. It'll really be fine being a hero and I bet Brother Barker won't even twitch an eyebrow when he finds out about Joel being the president of the Daredevils. And I'll be the vice-president now, myself." Amber smiled, remembering Joel's promise.

"Ooh, but I shudder to think what would have happened to us if Joel hadn't skipped church. Dadgum! And what if he hadn't made Pig go get Deputy Jack but tried to rescue us himself instead? We'd all have been dead ducks. No wonder Joel had acted so cotton pickin' brave! He knew perfectly well that men with guns and badges were on their way to really rescue us."

Amber tossed restlessly on the tangled sheets. "Thank the Lord that gosh awful red-headed man is stashed away in jail," she said to herself."There are certain drawbacks to living a life of danger. Poor Mother looked like she'd been dragged through a meat grinder, she'd been so worried. But, oh, I'll be so happy to own that little pup Pig's promised me, just soon as it gets weaned from it's mother. I better hurry up and get it while Gran's in such an obliging mood. Oh me, I can't hardly wait for morning time to come so's I can tell Carey Ann and Alta May all about——"

But before she had finished the thought, Amber Wellington, Daredevil, had fallen asleep.

ST. JOHN'S LUTHERAN
ELEMENTARY SCHOOL
"*For a Christ-Centered Education*"
3521 Linda Vista Ave.
Napa, California